About the Author

Christoph Burmeister spent his childhood exploring nature that inspired him to develop a vivid imagination from an early age. He studied Creative Writing at Cambridge University, then started a small copywriting business. His first novel, *The Poetic Murderer*, was published in January 2018, two years after he began writing it.

A year later, he received a scholarship for writing at the San Cataldo Foundation, Italy.

From this period, a very interesting novel emerged, where quantum physics meets human consciousness blending dreams and reality. Olympia made him an immediate offer. Christoph's right hand is the instrument of his daily writing routine.

Forever Young
A Quantum Fiction

Christoph Burmeister

Forever Young
A Quantum Fiction

Olympia Publishers
London

www.olympiapublishers.com
OLYMPIA PAPERBACK EDITION

Copyright © Christoph Burmeister 2021

The right of Christoph Burmeister to be identified as author of this work has been asserted in accordance with sections 77 and 78 of the Copyright, Designs and Patents Act 1988.

All Rights Reserved

No reproduction, copy or transmission of this publication may be made without written permission.
No paragraph of this publication may be reproduced, copied or transmitted save with the written permission of the publisher, or in accordance with the provisions of the Copyright Act 1956 (as amended).

Any person who commits any unauthorised act in relation to this publication may be liable to criminal prosecution and civil claims for damage.

A CIP catalogue record for this title is available from the British Library.

ISBN: 978-1-80074-126-3

This is a work of fiction.
Names, characters, places and incidents originate from the writer's imagination. Any resemblance to actual persons, living or dead, is purely coincidental.

First Published in 2021

Olympia Publishers
Tallis House
2 Tallis Street
London
EC4Y 0AB

Printed in Great Britain

Dedication

To Anna

Acknowledgements

I want to thank my mom and dad for everything. You're the best. Furthermore, I want to thank my sister, friends who have been there, my lovely girl and everyone on my publishing team. Thank you!

Chapter I
MS FOND OF THE BOTTLE

As you drink, you shall be. The party is always in full twerk, whichever way one looks at it. Ill-memory and loss of years have given me a name: Master Fond of the Bottle. A wealth of wit afforded me an education of extraordinary depth, depth of the human psychology and a crank turn of mind enabled me to sport a rich style; a fertile invention which early study of adulthood enhanced. Beyond all decency, the study of German philosophers gave me great pleasure too, not for the sheer force of vanity but from the ease; the kiwi-plush tickle and the poetry with which my eloquence gathered courage to unmask the evil twin within all polarity. I would like to contend that I have often been blamed for the nullity of my genius; a deficiency of scheme and savvy has been reason for much laughter and the study of Nietzschean 'Narcissism' serviced my opinions with notoriety. Indeed, a heavy, sad sack has burdened my shoulders — I admit, of which a soul is made, shoulders my step further down the road of indulgence — I revise — pours the glass half full, once it is half empty. Upon a one in all, whose measure shall be taken as less or more liable than my own, for to be courted with knowledge in the making of truth means by itself, weathering the Fata

Morgana which nestles on the untrodden path. If thus distinction permits that much, such as one of many subdivisions of a blackberry, this drupelet of my imagination shall be tasting sourly sweet to the fancy of thy mind.

After many years spent on deck, aft the engines of the past, I sailed in the age of twenty-seven — from the port of Hamburg, under the guise of The League, on a voyage through unknown waters to the port of Copenhagen. I stowed away aboard a ship — being driven by the itch for the remote, seduced by the sea, the restless up and down of waves and the ripple of laughter, which haunted me as childhood fever.

Our vessel was an early, round, unsound cog of about a hundred tons, with a single mast, open hull, built at Amsterdam of oak and could be rowed on short distances. She was freighted with jute and hemp from the Asian lands. We had also on board, Romanian spelt, Japanese seaweed, Mexican avocados, Indian ginger, Californian almonds, Garden pumpkins, Baltic herring and a few heaps of acai and goji berries. The stowage was messily done and consequently, offered space to stow away fairly easy, while the richness of superfoods sustained my health throughout the entire voyage superbly.

We shipped out with a mere nudge of wind, gathering little momentum, like a child farting in a swimming pool to accelerate and for many days, stood along the coast of Helgoland, without a rope to heave or a toast to roast, the monotony of the uncertain waiting soon ferried the first heap of goji berries — up for grabs and down my throat. The sea seemed chill. I sat along the hills of food and fibre and let the fancy for a cold beer and a hot fling become the imperative mood, so that my imagination drew for several days, all sorts of scenes before the inner eye.

One evening, lying drowsily behind a heap of acai, I observed (with eyelids souterrain) some sort of a lady passing by the clumsily piled rows of fibre. A fine tang of bergamot perfume reached after the nose. At first, I was astounded, nevertheless discounted the occasion to a mere product of my imagination and turned my mind back to fancy. But then, after a first beer can was emptied, as I heard someone snacking on something, smacking eloquently, my eyes gained superiority over the flood of pixel that centred in the vision. I stood up as quietly as possible and went behind the nearest row of fibre, scanning thoroughly the stowage. But she — the lady I believed I had seen, was already gone. I watched attentively the door until sunset, for a sign of her return, albeit my position was infinitively clear and I had to be careful, like a fish in foreign waters, not to be discovered, ending up dead in the shave-grass. Through a crack in the planks shone light which made the dust dance vividly on a bright shoal before my eyes and gave reason to peek, once in a while, upon deck where busy feet were hasting back and forth. My notice was soon afterwards attracted to a serrating, tobacco-troubled voice, commanding loudly. Some sort of a 'Captain', wearing knee-ripped jeans and a 'Shrimp Bizkit' cap askew, shouted stoutly, "Hoist the sails!" The crew was undergoing a rapid change of state from leisure to full tilt, toiling as the wind seemed to lengthen its arms. Although I believed myself comfortably safe at the bottom of the cog, yet (hours later), the ship begetting the sea in twelve knots quite shook me up. The air now became fan-askingly hot and was loaded with a whiff of rotting herring. As night arrived, dressed my mind in shades of hey-what-the-fuck-are- you-doing-here and the entire adventure of stowing away, faded in the bestial funk of rotting fish. The torch of my smartphone had died long since and the night-altered, owl-like perception enhanced the planks' sombre cracking. After years of resistance, enjoying a bottle bonanza, drafting from the philosopher's tap golden comfort and a severe amnesia causing a defect of memory, returned now the remote feeling that something was missing — the community of The League. Doubts studied me. Was I alone on this voyage? Where's the rest of The League? And, above all, who am I? Why am I here? At last, I had only a little time left and therefore, I opened myself to the strange rift between me, myself and I... decided to write those three questions down on a crumbled piece of paper (from my wallet) and keep it with me until I genuinely could answer all of them:

Who am I?
Why am I here?
Where's the rest of The League?

As the (still audible) captain said he could not detect any indication of danger, he ordered a jute bag of hipsters to inspect the heavy fouling on the rudder before the mainstream was reached. No watch was set and the crew was distracted by Facebook and Snapchat, stretching arms and legs upon deck. "Oh, Young & Wild, I am swimming in a lake of rosés," said Remember My Name, light-heartedly.

"I would kill now for a gin-soaked gelato," Young and Wild consented.

I went up the creaking ladder — not without risk to persevere my incognito. Indeed, my undertaking was causing the fine hairs on the neck standing erect. I told myself to walk back while I reached the last step of the noisy ladder; fear to be caught grabbed after my vigorously pumping heart and left me doubting for a moment. By force of habit, I fetched my smartphone to check for calming trivialities but was instantly reminded that Instagram was light a weight on this voyage I had embarked upon. My uneasiness, however, was balanced by a tremendous urge to peek upon the sea, feel the blowing of the wind ripple my hair, the Viking-like longing for the primal power address and although I retreated at first, at midnight I went upon deck. As I placed my first foot upon the ladder, I startled by a fierce, bursting noise — someone had farted aloud. A few baked bean cans were scattered around deck and implied that the chemistry of the air was bio. After ascending, the vision took shape and before I advanced further, I peeked at the wise sea. In the next second or so, the sea's tongue licked swiftly like a lizard over deck and severely caught my stand, so that I was taken away sternwards.

The lizard-like licking of the sea proved, in a rising measure, the loose ends of the cog. Although, not water-logged yet, as the mast had broken asunder, after a minute, sanctioned by the sea and, impromptu forsaken by the crew, who was out of sight, she sailed onwards.

By what miracle I had been kept on deck, entangled at the cog's rail at the stern, it is impossible to say. Completely drenched by the soak of Fernet-Branca, I disentangled from the rail and found myself upon recovery, jammed in between the raging sea and hipsters below deck (if they were not awash). With shaky legs, I gained my step and, looking somehow water-welted round, at a peek through a bull's eye, was instantly being struck by the mere fact that I was stuck on a cog among hipsters and their otherworldly vision: so urban, so fresh, so Ray Ban, beyond the wildest imagination — they were hiding from the sea under deck and playing Sudoku in their ragged denim, so that the reach after the bottle was again a decent reaction. I went under deck to the stowage, for I knew a few bottles of beer were to be found there. After thirsty-six sips, I heard the voice of the 'Captain', who had been misinterpreting the state of the climate on an epic scale and now, was trying to re-establish his rank by posting boldly videos and photos of the wrecked cog all over social media. Promptly, the crew uttered boos and dislikes at him with all their strength, calling him a 'douche with the swag of a bag potatoes'. Later on, all went back on deck, with the exception of myself, as the sun returned. I heard the 'Captain' accusing some sort of a lady of being a bitch, 'banging and swinging like a door', trying to reinforce his personnel support. But that backfired, as several girls were now quarrelling loudly, separating from the 'Captain's' view very proudly. The cog, however, without further assistance for the little security of it, was floating without navigation on the sea and our voyage turned into a random adventure, paralysed by the momentary risk of going down. Our Wi-Fi signal, of course, sustained competently, or we should have been struck by a hurricane of instantaneous fury. We sailed with laissez-faire velocity before the sea and the water currents clearly ridiculed us for our unknowingness. The framework of our stern was excessively plastered with unicorn stickers and in almost every aspect, we had neglected security measures for the sake of looking the better online; but to our extreme luck we found us miraculously afloat and that we had tons of organic vegetables at our disposal, shifted attention away from the unstable ballast of that cog's motion. The mere fact that the striking blow was now over and the crew apprehended little danger from the soothing wind, snacking sustainably on organic carrots and apples, well-believing in the lasting effect on nature's violence; we should inevitably gain such fair countenance that all lobster blush and herring glisten like sterling silver, in the tremendous swell which would ensue. But this green justice seemed by no means to be soon verified. (For we were all eaten up by trivialities, nothingness, nothingness that in an instant could become something and all of a sudden, would be all for us — the herd animal was (still) pretty tall a class, yet not so obvious but rather, masked by oblivion, oblivion present at an eminent extent.) For entire four days and nights — during which I drank persistently at a slowing rate, shot up all kind of thoughts about the outcome of this voyage; its fortune or misfortune and influence it could have on the rest of The League; like mushrooms networking invisibly in the underground, moss likely remaining in shady areas. Our course for the four days was, hardly distinguishable, with the sparse information that reached me, Sylt and Jutland by Ribe; we must have run by the west coast of Denmark. On the fifth day, the stench of the rotting herring became extremely haunting, although the wind that whistled through the cracks in the planks circulated relentlessly round. About noon, the crew was playing minority quartet. The sun shone impartially. Clouds were castling. A gay laughter once in a while reached out to the ear, as the 'Captain' put in a trump card to strengthen the own position on the back of everyone else and bottles popped with lustre. Seagulls flew by, emitting noise and dropping welfare bombs. Bitches! The taste of the goji berries grew insipid. Just before sinking into a deep sleep, alone, depressed and weeping, breathing the herring air, it dawned upon me some undeterminable power. It was dimmed, it forced me to think — what was it that The League had employed my service for? I waited in vain for the arrival of the voyage's aim at the sixth day — that aim to me had not arrived — like a Birkenstock sandal had always stepped on the quirky spot until it turned mainstream.

Henceforth, we were wrapped in green mist, so that we could not have seen an object at an arm's length distance from the cog. Eternal fog continued to envelope us, all anchored in the dark sea that fouled up the crew's temper. I observed too, that although the tempest in the mug continued to swash up and above the rim, there was no longer to be discovered the enormous need to peek at the phone as the deep desire to arrive at the port of

Copenhagen, freshened and attended me. All around were fear and thick dimness and a bearded gravity of colour. Superstitious horror surfed on the crest of waves into the spirit of our souls broken and my own soul was wrapped up in silent wonder. The crew neglected all care of the cog as worse as woodworms and securing ourselves, as well as a shot in the leg, to the rump of the broken mast, I looked out into the bitter world of the agitated ocean. We had no need for yolo or swag, nor could we form any guess of our situation. We were, however, well alight in the present moment of time (never not now) and felt great amusement of not meeting with the mercilessly manipulation of your corporation. In the meantime, every moment threatened to be dead — life was just yet and mounting waves hurried to overwhelm us. The swell surpassed anything that I had imagined possible, lifting on deck the slack waters of the past. My notice digressed by the lightness of my belly; by the lightness of those berries and reminded me of the excellent qualities of The League; but at the bottom of our cog, I could not help noticing the utter helplessness of help itself and prepared myself to disembark at any instant, for that death lingered in the creaking and cracking planks, at every turn, as with each knot, the swelling of the deep sea darkened my imagination appallingly. At a time, the crew asked the 'Captain' of what were to do, as the clue stone got tossed overboard long since and left us in a watery hell, where the air grew fishy and no heir but a 'Fear no more' seemed to unite us.

We were at the bottom of the spiritual abyss, when a late tweet from the 'Captain' broke loose a wave of laughter on deck. Waiter! One covfefe, please! tweeted he benevolently, like a baby bird gets kicked out of the nest into an unknown world and learns to fly. As he tweeted, I became aware of our dull, old language that could not enchant any more, like a chewing gum chewed. Closing my eyes outwards; opening my eyes inwards at a terrific light I glanced directly, as I beheld a spectacle upon the very verge of my reverie, of perhaps a whole week now. And it spoke to me brightly, affecting a tone of fatherly advice:

Radiant Light.

Being but man, proud man, captured in a little aquarium as fish hemmed in from all sides, seeing the other with a governor's eye. But the self is played on such a fantastic trick as makes nature weep.

Although dazed and confused by the Radiant Light's speech, the 'Captain's' tweet still exceeded that excitement, as it marked a new language in the making that we were about to embark upon. A single row on the keyboard for the 'Captain', a multitude of open ports to head into for a whole species. But what mainly inspired me with horror and astonishment was, that he yielded a hoard under the press of the savage sea and that ungovernable hurricane of egomania.

At that instant, I knew not fully and yet, what a sudden self-possession benefitted my ragged spirit! Left in self-awareness as far aft as I could, I awaited dauntlessly the ruin that was to overwhelm us — haste distorts the face! Our cog was at a slight tilt not ceasing from her keeling and slightly sinking, with her head to the sea. The intrusion of the descending mass struck her, consequently, in that unwelcome measure of her frame which was already under water and the inevitable partaking was to hurl me, with inescapable violence, into the rift of the stranger.

As I stumbled, the cog bent atilt and the crew panicked by the Pisa-like leaning.

And to my confusion ensuing its course lest nature's warnings would turn out ultimate. Unnoticed, I made my way to the rudder, which was partially broken and soon found an angle of steering myself for The League's sake. Rain poured in bucketful freshness, challenging our wits. Why it did so I can hardly tell. An indefinite sense of humour, which at first sight of the original navigators of the cog had taken hold of my mind, was perhaps the rescue of my sinking. I stopped drinking. I was willing to trust myself with an unknown bunch of people who had neither given me a name, nor taken a plaice from our waters, to shape a pivotal language of novelty and transcending aesthetics, inter-connecting plants, animals, humans and all other beings into One League. I therefore had thought proper to contrive a hideaway in the stowage of the cog. This I did by disguising my true intentions, in such a manner as to afford me a convenient retreat between the rows of fibre of the cog.

I had scarcely begun my work, when a footstep on the ladder leading down to the stowage forced me to make a first use of it. Some sort of a lady passed by my hideaway (behind a heap of goji berries) with an elegant gait. I could not see her face but had a chance to observe her silhouette. There was an inkling of great empathy, respect and understanding. Her aura uttered a load of laughter and her entire countenance cast light upon a dark ocean under the planks, quivering from the burden of this gravitational pull. I uttered to her, in a strong, determined tone, "Come noser! Come noser! I want to smell you something!"

Her smile brightened the sky, so that her rare flower appeared in full bloom. She had the merry sincerity of a Bronze Goddess. A sunny fragrance of bergamot, mandarin, vanilla and warm amber framed her fair appearance. With awe-inspiring eyes, she glanced into mine and instantly straightened my back. Her name was Anna Ivy, she said. From one second to the next, without any explainable reason, all my fears had disappeared. Not far from Copenhagen we went at length off the wrecked cog (rowing out in a lifeboat), turned around one last time and smiled, before the crowd ashore swallowed us up and swept us down in its flow.

Chapter II
THE BLACK-SCARAB

What woods? What scarabs? That bitches have been bitten by the witch fever.
— Eik Q. Lowend.

Midway upon the journey of my life I found myself within a forest dark, for the linear pathway had been lost. Here I acquainted with an Eik Q. Lowend. He was of an ancient Bernadotte family and had once been wealthy; but a series of misfortunate sport bets had reduced him to want. To avoid further distress from bookmakers and broken bonds, he left Kalmar, the city of his family's roots and cut the connection to his residence at Åland Island, near Åland's zoo, home to turtles, tigers and tourists.

This island is a very slim archipelago. It consists of little else than sheep grazing on small islands, migratory birds and some desolate rocks. It is separated from the mainland by deeply indented bays and fjords, which form excellent sheltered harbours for vessels of draught not exceeding nineteen feet. The surface of the island is generally rocky and the topsoil thin but, indeed, also containing many meadows that are home to a luxuriant variety of insects, lately invaded by the black scarab of the genus altum fearera. The vegetation, as might be supposed, is a combination of moss, meadows and miniature oaks. No trees of any magnitude are to be found here. Near the western coast, where some tourists during summer, by the climatic spas of Alby and Goodbye Russia stroll about, pass sheep, a line of hard, white beach, was covered with a dense population of the foreign black scarab. The sea here often attains the sympathy of both sun and moon, wrestling with the tide's conscience. Dark times of violent wuthering as well as bright skies and the feel of the sea breeze on your cheeks are both to be expected thus.

In the near distance, not so far from the white western beaches, Eik. Q. had built himself, on a small island, a small, cave house, which he occupied, when I first learnt about his peculiar conduct. This soon ripened into the strangest suspicion, for there was missing any hint of decency in his manners. He seemed to be very lonely and habitually disgusted by any apparent foreignness. It was a novelty that someone visited him and by no means a grateful one.

I had arrived, thrown off my raincoat, took rest on an armchair by the cracking logs of the chimney and tried to remove a slender sliver of wood from my finger that pained and attended me. Albeit, this strange splinter continued to sabotage my finer spirits, I waited patiently for the arrival of the man of the house, in hope that he would have a tweezer get it out easily. A few bottles of Falcon Stout were already in sight, to soothe the pulsating nerve endings. Hence, I drinkdrankdrunk and looked out into the dark, abyssal void of time and memory lost from the years in ego-slavery. The past seemed hazed and blurry. A frosty shiver crept up my neck as I tried to recall why I am here. With a fresh, slipping sound, enormous silver snakes sped through the garden of the house, through the grass and along the angelic sands. Wagner was played.

Soon after eight, Eik Q. Lowend arrived. As I slowly roused from my light daydreaming, a semi-bitter welcome, minted for one occasion — to tickle out my littler spirts — flavoured our encounter with a tang of ungenuine adventure. "Do you know where the fuck you are?" Eik Q. Lowend screamed in a fit of temper, grinning indistinguishably, whether in anger or embarrassment, from ear to err. His spare hair was — like the forest — withered at the top; and his neck was a swamp of dark freckles. A sharpened knife with a carrying rope trailed from his right hand and except for a pair of torn military shorts, he was naked. He closed his eyes, raised his head and breathed in heavily with swollen nostrils, assessing the current of warm air from the chimney for information. He coughed heavily and red spots in his eyes were a sign of diabetes. The forest and he were very ill.

I was puzzled by his erratic approach and looked out into the wild; as I arranged my thoughts, an attentive cloud paused for a while in its course; and then a slender wren with rounded wings befriended with a fencepost. I sensed those musical ties between the speeding snakes in the rain and his grief-ridden face, which would give a shudder when I pressed my pulsating fingers together. Then I realised that everything in the world was a medley of ghostly particles comprising different kinds of compositions: the woods, the rain and the pain of not knowing what's really going on... All was unified, equivalent and true. Simply, what you see. Finally, I answered through the ether:

"Look at the little river from the mountain and you'll know — my name is like water and down it comes, with the impulse of the stream." Eik Q. Lowend caressed thoughtfully his beard. It seemed to be a bit weird to evoke such a moment by reaching backwards in time, to create a history appropriate with our strange encounter of the now.

"Hm, I see, you are like me — Nature's son," he responded, seemingly appeased. Reckoning that I was speaking to him in a familiar tongue, he calmed quickly and beginbeganbegun to unravel the objects of his pity were the forms and phases of the island's swiftly altering nature. He had studied the unknown beetle from the beach, forming an ugly opinion about it and, more than this, he had premièred a promise by the portrait of his beloved grandad: that he would hunt the black pest down and wipe it out of their dear wildwoods. So far, so frightening.

I found him partially-educated, with a perverse obsession for the occult powers of mind but infected by a fear of the unknown and subject to misanthropy and melancholy. He had hoarded many books of national history, crowd psychology and ambiguous narration; and on a pedestal, right below a fabulous drawing of Nordic landscapes, stood erect a perfectly preserved version of *Mein Kampf* but he rarely read. Perhaps this was not only worrisome but hinting at a greater threat. The delusional whip of wetiko was whipping world-wide. Something was rotten on this island and I was taken astray. This place was strange. The shadowy symbols showing since my arrival, dazed and confused me. But something beyond patterned perception made it feel highly important too. That's why I decided to stay and see what I could learn from this strangely magnetic encounter. The game was afoot.

"What'd happened to those scarabs from the woods?" I asked, rubbing my eyes in disbelief, as I saw a myriad of corroded scarabs supine on the floor, which he (apparently) had injected with a mixture of aggressive acids.

"What woods? What scarabs? These bitches have been bitten by the witch fever!" Eik Q. suddenly screamed in his most deep, persuasive voice, as if he had to persuade himself about the sanity of his choices made. And he went on, now completely unchained:

"You see, it's because our enemy makes use of illegal weapons. Furthermore, our course is supported by leading artists and intellectuals. It's a holy war against the foreign plague. But hey, how could I make myself look the better, if I didn't even know someone was coming to visit me? Stay here overnight, my New Friend," he demanded explicitly and, "I will make you understand the whole picture."

"Not so sure, really. Tell me, what's the matter with this beetle? Is it invasive or what makes it such a threat to local nature?" I asked, already a bit scared, trying to maintain a sincere tone of voice.

"It's a scarab, you dumb. See, surely you won't get a full grasp of things tonight." Eik. Q. nodded self-assuredly, with a long, dark nose hair dangling from his right nostril, lingering over the question for ten minutes or so... But he didn't elaborate further. The unaesthetic hair dispersed an air of distrust in his words. Surely, there was some shit he hid.

The scarabaeidae was of a brilliant black like the starless sky — about the size of El Dorado plums — with a shimmering variety of facets for the mystery of it. "You never saw a more angst-inducing creature than the scales emit but of this you cannot judge properly, until you've filled your stomach with the delicacies that will this way come. I ordered a ton with this brand-new App by Drone — EatMySon. 'Til then help yourself with a few pecans." He looked for some nutcracker in the drawer but found none, mumbling something obscure. I did not hear the exact words but I could guess their cynical charge, which would grow absurd and somehow spherical when I tried to listen more closely.

At length, he drove out his breath in a long sigh. He looked over to me, sitting in a vino-red, vintage chair, still stunned by the mass murder of those scarabs. They were deep-set eyes that seemed in the light of the stranger, like dark circles with slight glimpses of madness. Then he flipped his tongue upside-down, licked his brittle lips and scanned the uncommunicative corridor. Erratically, he then stole forward and cast like a stone throw kitchenwards without any detectable emotion or word spoken. It was as if he was physically present, yet mentally absent. The silence of the dark forest had a calming effect, while continually imbalanced by the odd acts of Eik Q. and at this hour of the day, there was not even a bus going back to town, if things would turn out ultimate crazy.

At midnight, the food arrived and filled my stomach prematurely, as much of my appetite had vanished with time spent near the dead scarabs. "Done?" Eik Q. asked with measured tongue, glancing at my half-full plate.

"Thanks," I said and, "I've had already a few stouts and my stomach strikes at this ungodly hour." Moon smiled like it meant it, thus changing the way supper appeared on the oaken table into gloomy news. Underneath the table, the carpet of dead black scarabs, which he believed were a bad omen for all of us but in respect, to which he wished my opinion not before sunrise.

"Co-co-uld youuuu d-d-d-rive me b-b-back to town, I have some unfinished business in the-e-e-ee pub?" I stuttered suspiciously, played by dark impulses, adopting a feeble tone of voice.

"If only I had expected you in a timely manner!" said Lowend, "And how could I foresee that you — the dreamy dude coming out of the forest, would turn into such an impossible man and now, as we slowly befriend, wants to escape!" Discomfort seemed to grow in him. He went on. "You see, as I was coming home, I met Master B — from The League on the way and, not without intention to upset you, I handed over all materials I had gathered on the scarab and gave him my truck; so believe me when I say that, I can't give a detailed report today and you are stuck until his return next morning! But what must be said: The loss of native insects on Åland Island continues at an alarming rate, ecosystems are terribly out of balance and we need any helping hand we can find. If we don't do stuff, it might be soon too late for all of us. The plague spreads rapidly. So, stay here overnight, I mustn't say it twice," Lowend demanded, by raising his voice to a pre-apocalyptical pitch.

"Well, all right, enough for today," said I, inauthentically like likes on social media. But, damn, he had become such an ugly man within two hours or so, with nicotine-stained moustache and dirt under his fingernails. A history of misfortune and anger dwelled in his delusional eyes. And, from my conversation with him, I too learned to speak in code, to interpret his unspoken signs and the inflections of his voice, never to ask too much and, above all, never to comment too much on what he said. By being shapeless like water, I could swim along the width of his contemptuous ocean of comments without persevering my incognito and still be potentially overwhelming like tides, if needed. He had put his long sharp knife on the table like a threat, which had re-entered my perception. The seed of leaving him at any opportune moment was planted, as unwitty weeds had crept into the pauses of his speech, overgrowing like shadows the width of his countenance.

Far off the patterned path of perception, I had to decide… Two roads diverged into the knowing woods — one beset by darkness and one liberated by light… And sorry, I could not travel both… For as I'd made up my mind about which path to take, broke my pen suddenly asunder and forced me to stop writing. An abrupt ending to all hope that we would ever become something like friends — the mysterious voice of fear in my head and I…

…After taking a deep breath, I closed the door of the gloomy cave house shut and not turning around, left Eik Q. behind to experience the interiors of Åland Island's woods alone and colour my own opinion. Goodbye to the outgrowing, long, dark nose hair of despair!

Soon the house was out of sight and in the rear, the wonderful woods were gained again and I strolled slowly before the moonlight, looking for a safe and solitary place to spend the night.

Such a freshness was wafted across the oaks and limes that I felt pity for the cold darkness creeping out of the margins beside the path alit. I trod the lean forest floor, wandering like frogs, my feet shuffling over the moss and climbing over the slippery logs with as much pleasure as the bright moonshine. At length, I camped along a gentle stream near the tranquil sea. Put to a level between earth and canopy I observed (to my astonishment) with such reverie the wilderness unfurling.

Half awake, half asleep, dreaming of my dearest love, one single star glimmered through the blanket in the sky. Perhaps at midnight, one was awakened by a wolf's howling (wolves were re-populating Sweden) or a shrilly cricket sitting on one's shoulder and was lulled to sleep again by the streamlet's purling. It was pleasant to lie like a seven in the low grass, curling like morning dew on a maple leaf into the metaphysical world. It occurred to me a thousand thoughts knocked on the door of consciousness but none of them was admitted, as I drifted off dreamlandwards.

In the wake of the next day — a radiant light spoke to me, so truthful in its finitude, pouring forth the cup of epiphany, as if it had been waiting for its chance to colour my consciousness the whole night, months, years, perhaps even lives.

Radiant Light.
You're on a journey,
A journey to find out the truth. This journey leads you Inevitably to the reunion:
The reunion of men and machine.
We create the new human, We create the humachine; Your spirit wounded.
By the war of consciousness forms the best basis for this —
Only he who had suffered long enough knows the abysses of the soul so profoundly.
That the will
Makes the damaged soul insensitive and so, free from pain and fear...
Do you want to lead us from darkness to light?
To youth, to light.

Then idle time went slyly by and left me smiling broadly. The sea, the sun and all's well in the flow — a swan's a-swimming softly. I must now go and extend my world as much as migratory birds must fly to wintering grounds. My name, it shall be said at last, Jon Known, was carved into the old oak growing by the little streamlet, of which I learnt a-following:

An acorn obeys its own laws, falls off the tree and springs and grows and flourishes as best it can, perchance it outgrows the shadows of its fellow trees to be closer to the sun. If a plant cannot live according to its nature, it dies; and so does a man eaten up by his own shadow; feeding his appetite to the morbid.

Chapter III
GREEN GIANT SNAIL

I look out and the tree grows in me. I'm beset by worries and in me, stands a house.
— Jon Known.

This is a delicious day, when the whole presence is one sense and delight seeps through every pore. I spot and adore a strange liberty in nature, a liberty of herself. As I walk along the path of the park's pond, pondering the cool as well as casual wind and I see the frog jump from the fire into the water, all the elements are unusually harmonic to me. At the stone shore, a socially awkward lizard tries to trump his fellow lizards by differing in tail size and the note to the grey heron is borne in the wind, patterning over the rippling water. Sympathy for silence as willow and poplar leaves properly prime my breath for the present moment; yet, like the pond, my merriment is rippled but not wrestled. These small waves run smoothly through the horizontal sunrise in tandem with my heart-throb. Though I'd sought not silence, it is the gentle wind in the breeze of the moment that lulled me to sustain in rest. It is like music, jazz do it: repose. Though the repose is rarely the ground of the human play. The wild animal does not repose but seek their prey in the now; there, outdoors, a treasure is hidden in the silver trails of the green giant snail. They are nature's courses — routes which connect the days of real life takes place outside!

MR HORST HORSE sat at the table on his own. He ate with zest the lettuce alone (him and his phone). The overwhelmingly eager waiter, Walter Wit — Good Morning, Mr. Horse! — left to pursue his very profession: waiting. He had no faith in himself and would probably wait forever for something in his life to change for the better.

Horse liked to indulge in wishful thinking while he devoured the dishes of the HAPPY PIG. Most of all, he liked pasture grass in liaison with flaxseeds and fresh fruit but no garden refuse. It's truly cruel how much good stuff restaurants throw away at the end of the day (must the dumpster-diver have thought before he disappeared in the container). Although the amounts were not trivial, Horse didn't give a fig. He always ate up his plate. Free from worry, feeling rich, 888, he thought he was thinking, for which he felt smart and super-sensitive, almost like a poet really.

The horizon was reddening.

Another breath: taken. He breathed consciously as a way of mediating the ongoing chaos in the mind. Brain left, brain right. The rhythm of his breath was reminiscent of Coltrane changes — making him see things from a variety of perspectives. Cup of tea, now: mental ass kick. Promptly crossed the street. A pungent tang of urine hung provokingly in the air. There! Asquat, two gurls peed between two parking cars, producing the curls of a meandering river. Can do it me too. Assumed a position of gender equality.

Entered Café Open. Closing: zippered up. Door met doorstopper. A horizontal study of heads. Travelling faces in unknown places. Examined today's papers. Sno. Wing. In. No. Man's Land. More than just a headline. Brain: connecting dots: to whom it may concern. Feminism: Mary Nobody killed her husband Captain Ahabibi with a gigantic dildo. Wandering eyes. Read backwards. Stumbled over a c, badly. Then, the Daily Cartoon: a bird in the bush. WQNDFBS QE PFBCFPTLQN. Mind: A riot of roadrunners flashing by. Beep beep! Having the minimiminute of me like. Turned the paper to the other side. Unmounted: Swiss bag placed by the table's left legs. Ordered breakfast: Can I get a drip of milf into my coffee, please? I wouldn't recommend it, for our milk is very fatty and contradicts the fine notes of the coffee. Okay easy. Sat down at the unlabelled table that had always time. So refreshingly postmodern. It knew that I would come back, having studied horseraces and humans on cable TV for years.

Staying domestic: horses in the stable; humans by the cable TV. Thirst: first, then: pen to paper. Andy Arbeit, my frustrated, fantasy friend had arrived with a busload of ideas and asked me politely to start working. In came the waiter with a tray. Wondered what comes with the buns. Felt groggy. A hoppy beer would do miracles, no stout about it.

—Yeah, come on, bear! Liltingly, Walter Wit danced towards me with melting cheese and fried calamari in garlic sauce upon a plate for breakfast — it was better than expected.

—Serrano sunshine when she's gone, sounded from the speakers. Thinking summer: beaches, bikinis, bar-hopping — winter in Spain must be less straining. More sun, more fun. Where life won't be dim. At the sky, slim patches of clouds formed into three words: You Are Free! Tipped.

Listened to the music that twisted the system of my musing. Stupid, Cupid. No. A father's loss. Warm buns with butter, a shake of berry. It started to rain. Suddenly people were in a hurry. All comes with time. The rain's entourage: very welly. Wanted fresh water, pure. Best cure for thirst. 'Twas Thirstday: per se not a good day to stay sober for long. The beer was served promptly for a fine finish.

Back glued against the wall, head faced Mrs Well's back. A modern woman, with more money than most, men envied her for her strong arms. She bent forward to pick up a Polaroid picture which had fallen out of her purse. Assthetic view. Must do cross-fit or take the steps up to the fifth floor or more, oftentimes. Perhaps, she lifted weights too. Manish girl: biceps over boys. On quiet sneakers she walked off to the bar, paused for the lavatory door, then entered.

Meantime, a Volkswagen Multivan bred A BUNCH OF KIDDOS (noise!) in the periphery of the eye. It was cool like penguin: outside. The cold, wet wind whipped them in. Ending of the paragraph.

'—You don't want anything for breakfast?' asked the worried mother. Taking sides:

'—No.'

'—Well, is that so? Pancakes will do, hm: Eggbert, Wayne, Carlotta and Jeremy- Klaus-Cane, you gotta eat breakfast to grow tall and strong.'

What's right and what's wrong? One might say you're conditioned by convention.

Bundled attention: her see-through blouse. She did not want anything, everything for the kids. Was it true?

The cluekey to the clarityroom was beyond the cafécosmos. Her kids shovelled up the pancakes; she dug her own grave. Monogamy was her faith; promiscuity her latent fantasy; somewhere in-between dwelled the lesson. During the birth of her third kid her personal hunger vanished like a ghost. It demanded a loving devotion of her, ghosting out of the woods of her deepest desires. Food for the youth: He who eateth from the spoon, lendeth to the stool. Thus, spilled Zarathustra.

She rose early at 6 a.m., curling like mastic from Mediterranean trees. Her shoulders ached from carrying the boys into their beds. Dark circles around her eyes: on first name terms with. To understand the morning dew, that is, to be ready to die. And the perception carousel slid on!

There! The plain-clothed man with unkempt hair at the unstable table. A blind thread and needle in the hay. All day along the edge of the city. Looking for something to come from underground excursions. Like… a Russian spy. Drink vodka, play balalaika and care a bear. More or less polite encounter. Magnetic strangers. Either ends met at the bar.

—How dangerous are you from one to ten?
—Depends on the joy of pretending.

—You are handsome!

Handed her some kind of map to find the secret for eternal youth. 'Twas sketched on the back of the Polaroid picture. I had traded it from the strong lady for an unending waterfall of original ideas, which was a timeless embrace. Mrs Sputnik put it into her left boot, tears welling in her eyes and heaven growing a wildflower. What was on it? I'd promised, I wouldn't tell anyone.

Thick liquor was poured into a glass, twice. Must drink about the sense of... semiaquatic snakes. Life is short, art is anaconda. I came to play the cards as they were assigned to me. Novelty versus habit. Same, same but two ends: snake tail and snake head. Where do we head to?

A silent scream from the lavatory. The dreams I'd dreamt some years ego still affected my reality. We were together. It was better than anything ever before. That's all I can remember. Had smoked too much weed in my teenage, perhaps. Turned the page, maybe, sunken in thoughts. What did it all mean?

The news seemed blurry. The new shift had arrived in a hurry. A wanton waitress with fake rich-bitch-lips, giving her an air of despair to be deemed a lifeboat, served pretzel sticks with butter and a subtle knife. Micro-muffins with whipped cream wiggled into the vision too, north-west of the steaming coffee machine, and... phew... another film was full... put the lid on. Fast forward.

Highday night, after the concert with the Russian spy, had returned to her hotel. A strange urge to fling myself into the unknown had conquered and attended me. The sinuous path of lawns and parks did not permit exact determination about my lost love's origin. A rare flower had crossed my way. Wanted to grow side-by-side to her but my courage declined at the scent of her beauty. Time passed by mutely, disguising the truth. Must reach the other side of the city in a whiffy. Flying faster than Ali's fisty. Cash is clay. Walked over Pennybridge to save time is money is the currency of the ignorami; scanning the ground for pennies, head down, penny-pincher style. Carefully looked up... A video on YouTube: How To Be Single. But it was too many to watch, consuming the clock. So, you think then, gentle reader, Horst Horse was a lonely loser, a roistering coward? Well, read on.

You see, Horst Horse was active on Tinder — a modern design of Frankenstein in form of an application for your phone. So smart, so seductive, so stupefying. Damn, no matches. Later!

On Pennybridge's balustrade slimed a green giant snail beyond the trail of good-and-evil. It had a pale shell, shimmering skin and retreated its antennae, as strangers neared. The signal was explicit: lettuce alone — (me and my home). I nodded understandingly and gathered disarrayed information in the unsteady stream of consciousness. Underneath the bridge, two homeless hippies seemed just to have found a new dwelling place, telling tales about rude tourists dropping their plastic waste in their backyard. Not. In. My. Graffiti glossed on the grey walls.

—Whale: Done. Save. The.
—Shit. Cut. The. Bull.

—Eat pussy. Not animals.

Thought onwards: Priority sequence: Family: first. Friends: second. Thoughts: absurd. Followed Walter Wit's invitation to his family farm outside of the city. Sad under a chestnut tree. A post-modern moment: stillness. That's when the train of thoughts threatened to escalate. Well, that's okay but it in the end, it won't stop. A chestnut dropped on Horst Horse's head. He had to think (again) about the manifold meanings of this random walk.

What did really matter? Family? Friends? Fishing? National identity? Flying around the globe? Collect wild animals or stamps? Finding a beautiful girl? Marry? Adhere to an outdated ideal? Work hard, party hard? Clutch at a straw? Find a good bar and get drunk or a bench to read some more news in past tense? The latter or perhaps it's better to be pregnant with the moment? Truth is, we are free to dismantle all our old believes and advance to higher-self. It is never, ever too late. Whatever stage we are at. There's always higher-power and there's always higher-self. Good luck, me, myself and I!

Horse read the latest issue of Farmer's Digest on the phone. Hay press. Food for the cows. Head down, nose up. Ruminants with green thoughts. Outlook: from here to hay. To avoid the stench of life, that is, Sartre on rye. Not exactly what you would call a light snack. One first must go down, before one can lift-off: thermic forces. A clown and a helicopter. To propel revolution. Search and destroy: yolocaust. Bomb shitting, comma: tear in the flow, breaks the wave in an ocean of uncertainty. The League was operating in the underground. Silent as the tree in amber. Another can beer: opened. Cheers to the archetypes. Energy fields of influence elicited the fragmentation: living room of adhesive labels, scattered all around. Where's my mind? An ancient address hidden in a haystack. Needle. In. The. Want… To buy an apartment to be less hindered by corruptive energies, more home, more hermit, lonelier but her damn-it! A cosy place for me and my Wi-Fi — missed her mucho. Wireless fences, crippling senses. Was a senseless, transhuman, unconscious future ahead? The animal that therefore I am not any more. Derrida derailed? Smartphone: a portable prison cell, they say. 5G: a mission to hell, they say. Surveillance capitalism: People are more like statistics than actual human beings, they say. Twenty-five percent of the waking day wasted on the voidoscope, they say. Quarter to cyborg! Next on the agenda: Give me your heart feelings, they say. What's the plot here? Objective: The elimination of the habitat of a rare animal: the hipster. Nobody wanted to be one; but someone wanted to be… unique and free like a wild animal, living in peace. Freedom: was that a possibility?

The calm cows turned their heads to nature and chewed the cud. Cuddle a cow to heal, Farmer's Digest had suggested. Did so. Felt much better. Fell into a deep sleep on the pasture green. A little resting from The League's pressures. A dreamy dive into the fictional circuit of time shaped all equal. And then, ever falling deeper and deeper into the dark abyss of dystopian dreams, the brightest, most brilliant light spoke to me afresh, adopting a tone of fatherly advice:

Radian Light: You're on a journey,
A journey to find out the truth.
This journey leads you inevitably, to the reunion.
The reunion of men and machine.
We create the new human.
We create the humachine. Come with us
And conquer your fear; will disappear, for
All is One:
Daynight, Wintersummer, Warpeace, Satietyhunger
— Gettogether.
And fear no longer. To youth, to light

Chapter IV
HOMAGE TO PARIS

Paris... Crêpes Suzette, liberty and sex, yes... Here we go again!

As Jon Known stared out of the plane window at the blending clouds, he knew the next twenty-four hours or so would be his last ones.

Lift off. Two hours of sleep. A rough landing, quite concave... Yet, since all passengers survived — suddenly a quite convex change of moods... Oeuf.

New-born in the City of Light, registered at the Backpackers Hospital — BackHo, in Newtongue — was a startlingly different sort of speech, highly encouraged and taught in the School of Equality, ranked in the curriculum higher as Newton's theory of gravity.

At La Fontaine De Belleville: gravitated inside. To see and not to be seen, that is the attraction. Quick observatory glance, then action. Fish-eyed by the waitress: Miss.

Happened to be stumbling over a bowl with granola; filter coffee, black, lifting and firming, was flung through the air. A brown wave of despair emerged... Spread all over the floor; all over the world. Shock. Shame. Strange speed. Got the whole globe in my pocket, always available, indeed, feelings and beliefs could change the whole world immediately. Our daily routine: click, edit, and send.

To start the day with a happy ending, that is, to do something different than before. Dalíberation, he would be calling it later. Then, the waitress turned up the volume of the radio on floor foursome… Futuristic trumpets — guess what — carried up the humour. Lobsteresque laughter coming out of the glazed puddle on a pedestal in the middle of the pantry. The anxious animal that therefore, I am observed by a million cameras. Surveillance of the fittest. The deep state of an obvious super-structure was prone to perish but pregnant with potentiality. What's next?

Known read. The news: USB-stick found in a fox hound's year-old frozen faeces.

Whoosh! Little Hunger crashed right through of the window. Thus spoke Big Bill, the restaurant owner: the bigger, the better. Mia Wallet, however, suggested: the bigger, the sicker. Put into the litter: the news. Remembered: Since Galileo the world was divided in two: mind & matter. Now it was divided in three: mind and matter and madness. Was the latter deliberately planned by the one-percenters to gain global control over every individual on the planet? The League showed great progress.

Meanwhile, the waitress meddled with her smartphone. Reckoning this, Known felt followed by some dark force. Security cameras put him into focus. To accelerate the payment process, we settled somewhere in the zone of the unspeakable. Left her immediately thereafter, for I felt as if trapped in a Kafka story, hungering to death until only the skeleton of my individuation was left.

In spite of that, the waitress smiled like she knew that we would meet again. 'Til next time then, Madam de Pomelo, with the lush décolletage. Mystery tattoos on her arms, certainly charming.

Down in the street, little eddies of wind ferried dust and dead leaves and the sky a harsh, grey garden. There seemed to be no sympathy for colour. The city had chosen to wear a grey cape on that day but hey, only to make herself seem so much duller than she was. Paris — not the worst place to perish, of course.

Met Miss Laurie La Vid at café La Vida Loca. Kiss, kiss — one on each cheek. Busy feet shuffled over the street.

—All well?

—All well or Orwell?

Both of us smiled. Pale leaves lingered along the lime alley, curling in an abrupt rush of wind. The season's grand plan: To weed the garden of human neurosis, so that new roses could bloom therein. The light of her eyes dimmed. Some unspoken force truth- trimmed the course of our conversation. Pity, she had to leave so early. A fleeting glimpse of what may have been, shimmered symbolically on the splendid surface of the canal. A spinning bottle among the waves went wildly up and down. Silent laughter coming out. Then I knew, we were both too curious to give up our freedoms to settle down. Sounds made them wander off.

Back to no business: love, the profession of a full-time dreamer. Turned around on the heel of the moment mortal. Out, out and away. Made up my path to the padlock- be hung bridge. Graffiti: A Smurf leant on a King of Sweden. Why it did so is impossible to say, even here, in the incessant search of… Truth: a real demon at disguise. It has the structure of fiction. Went down that unspoken route. Street life, tarmac, gone massive. Pop-up obstacle, one step too far would be: in-Seine. Stay and study the ripple of the canal's current: steady flow, steady go, unlike the train in the brain had many junctions. The deconstruction of an outdated ideal proceeded to overcome the old paradigm.

Location: Rue de Lancry. Words in the mind: wiggling wet and wild like a lipstick. At Crêperie La Dérive, a construction worker wore a baguette on his head and danced to La Macarena. So real, brief beliefs, refuse la plastique. Rendezvous with yourself: selfie at Pierre's photo shop. A door in adorably azure trousers, unopened, closed zipper. The Promised Nevermind. Pigeons picked up treasures from the road's buffet is always open. Breadcrumbs with a Michelin star. A paradise for the punks of the air.

To others: simply the pest. Instead, sticking to bread: Nutella. She had a soft spot for it, he suddenly remembered to put an important letter into the post box. A message to massage MS Fond of the Bottle's messy mind. Read it one last time, then dropped it.

Would he ever find back to the pathless path of freedom?

Long time since the last riot in the roads. Here, in Paris, the streets were full of shit, always but storms were rare. People walked swiftly, as if their asses were itchy. A sign:

Cheese of The Day: Blue Monday. Bang! It stroke him in his periphery: Ice Ice Baby Smile Eat Love Drink Talk Share Lunch Kiss. Strange signs and symbols tried to seduce. However, the grass's gotten greener and grander, since the Broccoli Revolution had changed the way we think, he thought. The League's propaganda was still the most powerful among all mind manipulations.

A harmonica player jumped out of a manhole.

—What's the time?

—An eternal child moving pawns over the chessboard.

—Thanks, goodbye, I'm such a VUP (Very Unimportant Person) but persistent, positive and patient. A rosy pixel collage in your uncosy view. Fragrant French women in fire-red costumes hosted several seconds of my lifetime. Turned sexy: the moment. Persex, it's never too late to get laid. Perhope, see you later in Café Chameleon.

Where's that? Now, think before you act. The universe is like one big, juicy octopussy, reaching out its tentacles: to be shaken, that is, taking the risk of being seen in all beauty. The queer view of the real world unstirred.

Two smartphone addicts walked smartly ahead, smashing their heads against shopping windows. Mirror of the material mind. Led into a void. Up in the corner of a big building, Frankenstein peered furtively over the fence. A monster having the appearance of man hiding in a camera. Six quick swipes to the right. Home is where your phone is. Right. Do they know my sexual preferences too? Stinging smells rose from the sewer. Bonjour, nose! Better leaving sooner than later.

There! To the right side, an advertisement: Mango Butter Curls: promotion to the hair. But hair no more. Pity, another anthropomorphic concept made him feel like having a picnic. Permission to listen to the sick traffic at Port St. Martin was given by the mind patrol. Cars coughed passed; scooters screamed in between. Continued to binge-think a plurality of perspectives far off the social media scene.

A coral-like façade, unevenly tanned. Probably public property. Found, pass columns and a female gossip columnist, Nicolas Le Blanc, staring blankly to the ground. Not sure what he'd spotted. Perhaps, without maybe, a portal to a higher dimension. Not worth mentioning here, only the ego (excusez-moi, EGO) mattered! Ever onwards for the sake of The League's leadership, prone to perish. But not now, not here in Paris.

What walks best? Ask Shoenissimo! 2Shy to step inside. Really? No, it's closed.

Then again, it hammered in my head those persistent question: Who am I? Why am I here? Who are the other members of The League? I felt like chasing a ghost, walking on clouds. Less shoe, more you.

There, many perfumed men performed magic tricks on the pavement for free.

Cigarette. Mouth. Fire. Fume: You breathe in as you breathe out. Recognition is the first step to recovery. Boom! An airstream disengaged from the rear exit of an angry granny: sonic sentence. Time tugged on her eyelids hung superdown. Turning heads. Furious jury: A few pedestrians detested, looking at her with a tinge of disgust and turned around, as a sign of protest. But the majority passed by mutely, neither laughed nor detested, as The League had truth-vaccined them during the grand pandemic and thus, imposed total control over their wetiko-infected perception. Anywhat, I can't discuss this further atm. In search of cash threatened to be on the verge of extinction: walnut sentence. #Thinking, a hard nut to crack these days. Inkling, I had another idea. The material mind wanted me to buy coffee and cake and take photos and post those all over social media, as if somebody would care. They won't! Consequently, I moved to meet at Shakespeare & Company, an expatriate culture was fully abloom. Fleur-de-lit. Spring wanted to roll in like sushi but it's too early for this. It was Februweary, the postmodern beginning of wintertime. Time illusion. Check: 10.47 a.m. There, the eyes said to the mind — a bunch of rabbits fled from the pet shop to multiply, in search of the holy carrot. A surreal construction of the Ministry of Creativity. That's it, hopped on.

Reached Rue Du Bugs Bunny. 8-bit art at the walls: looked funny. Stopped abruptly! Red traffic lights. Nipples on the ground aided the blind. Reality revolutionised, shifted by a quantum jump.

Three black cats sat by the riverside. Walked backwards with eyes shut. Eiffel into oblivion. The three black cats by the riverside, ever unworried, wouldn't care a hair loss. Across the street, selfie scenes with béchamel-coloured tourists galore. Was Eye the observer or the observed?

Notre-damn! Many Instagrammers on fire. Must have been a nest somewhere nearby. Perhaps in the canopy of the tree of life is like a sequence of images that feed on likes. What is it like to be human? Strive or thrive?

Arrived at the charmingly lit bridge the chi flowed freely. No fences, no photos, no filters. Flowers grew wildly on a strip of meadow. Low noise levels now. A little wind kindly and soundly wrapped round the gestalt of moment. Stepped into the river of change. Caught by a blood-sucking thought: Eco > ego. What was really happening?

It was a cloudy afternoon in Februweary and the clocks were striking stale. The ducks were fed with white bread. My memories were melting but matter of fact is, everything is a matter of perspective… This land… Is not leas'd out… To a pelting farm… But cultivated with poetry. An artist's dream in Paris: dreamt into peril. Night arrived. A little sleep. Drowsed in in a hostel's group room. There's always one persistent snorer. But the light of the day reminded me to kindle kindness, which broke with bitter candles the light sleep of revenge.

A new day, a new view. Along the wind and waters, from the ether of his transforming presence was born, if it were, a polite… Farewell to Known. Another linguistic label: peeled off. Who was knocking on the doors of perception?

Guessed right. Salvador Aldí, his chest sensing the press from the cheap bottle of red in the inside pocket of his ripped Blue Valentine linen suit, slipped elegantly through the open door into the hall of Bibliothèque Mazarine, though, not unseen by the chief librarian who asked for his personal details, before she would assign to him a study place in the reading room. Number: sixty-three. Missionary Position. Listened to the signs that were given.

The hallway smelled of old books. This, he thought with a twinkling eye, this was good old, literary Paris, chief City of Amore, a more romantic space was only to be found here, in the freshest of the provinces of Lemonia, the atlas of his fantasy. He tried to squeeze out some juicy memory that should tell him the other provinces of Lemonia but those thoughts slipped out of his grasp. It was true what the scholars of The League had told him. Memories pass swiftly like lives!

It had also been suggested by the book he had just been taking out of the towering shelf that seemed to collapse like a building with a bad foundation, if he wouldn't have stood up immediately to do so. He'd been driven by a mysterious force. Why it did so happen, of course, I couldn't comprehend. It'd a crumbled texture to it and a bit yellow of age. It felt earthy, warm and gave off an odour of scooped cotton.

Then Salvador Aldí stopped painting quantum worlds with words, partly because he wanted to go to a party. He did not know what had made him pour out this stream of sound-making symbols. Who was behind all those thoughts? Perhaps he was inspired by the cheap, red wine. A child-like curiosity overwhelmed him while he was uprooting such a surreal sentence had formed itself in his mind, to the point where he almost felt equal to the felt sensation, so he had to write it down, despite his former intention not to. It was, certainly uncertain, because of this other incident of the farting granny that he had suddenly decided to come to Mazarine and begin to mother his dream. Grandmotherfart effect!

Although, unrest rose in him, he sat up straighter: his eyes re-focused on the piece of paper. Althoughts, he wrote them down without hesitation.

Imagine air. A barefooted bubble. Up, up and away. If you could, dear reader, perhaps the rumours of vast underground conspiracies were true after all — perhaps The League really existed and controlled the fade of the world! All depicted things happened — if, indeed, they did happen.

Faithfornication, they called it, when some person thought shit that wasn't for the sake of supporting the current belief system. Still the collective consciousness was transforming. The fake face of bad faith had faded, at least for a moment. On a banner of the Broccoli Revolutionists stood out in bold capitals: LET THE LEAGUE CEASE, LET THE LEAGUE CEASE, LET THE LEAGUE CEASE.

Perused my notes to find a clue what all this had to do with me. Thought, who was the leader of The League? An approximation: his penis was the meanest; his face so sourly tanned, he must have been kin to grapefruits of some kind; his skin was like a fringed carpet strewn with past sins; overall a meagre man but evil and, it was clear from his appearance that The League needed to be reformed before the warning of his rise to power would turn out ultimate. Of this, most people in contemporary

Paris were convinced, even if they did not know it yet. Then, to complete the fake media picture, the instrument of his choice was a voidoscope — a media instrument disguised as a telecommunication device, used for erasing painful memories, so that the crowd could live on in pleasurable servitude. This, he thought, with a sort of disgust, was the castrated reality of his past too. It was true. He had been given a multitude of names, in Newtongue: MS Fond of the Bottle, Jon Known and Salvador Aldí, among numerous others. Brief bubbles like those on the chat record of his phone. Somewhere or other they were still alive and habitually drinking beer or smoking marihuana cigarettes or merely sauntering around: perhaps somewhere, as conspiracy wants it, on Hawaii or beyond sea and islands, under the protection of ancient spirits, uncorrupted comrades of One League — like Tupac, William Blake or Shakespeare and the other worthy, perhaps even in Lemonia itself.

By refusing the terribly insipid force of The League, Salvador Aldí was advocating freedom of speech, freedom of thought and freedom of expression — and all this in a rapidly expanding tongue of spellbinding imaginations, which were a sort of parody of the habitual style of the current belief system. But there was the rub. There were those few old, uncorrupted comrades who just wouldn't bend their knees to the boundless greed of the ruling class; rekindling the spirit of a new, fairer generation.

Having written those, admittedly rather incoherent, thoughts down, he got up and moved out fast of Mazarine. Uninterruptedly, he walked and walked without a word, on and on, until he stood in the very middle of Pont Des Arts. The brisk wind kempt his dolphin hair as he climbed up the balustrade. There, he were — imagine it, dear reader — in full figure, with swelling chest and vigorously pumping heart, more alive than he ever had been before, in-sync with the wind, playfully leaping over each obstacle, since dancing back and forth, ever at danger to fall down into the ice-cold water, so in love he was with the music, the silent wonder of that precious moment of his life, appreciating it while it's still there.

From behind the bridge ahead, approached a ship atop the wild stream of the Seine — 'twas the barge Fortuna, in full steam; and since then… well, since then, he never has been seen again. The end of a castrated reality; the beginning of the new age of freedom, leisure and abundance. But still, who was with him on the other side? A sigh… and suddenly he realised that he was completely alone.

What was I doing out there? What was the meaning of this trip? Should I have been on a secret mission out here in the streets? Or was I just roaming around these cafés and bars and art galleries in a sort of mirage or had I really come out here to Paris to work on a genuine story?

I reached my pocket for the library card; 'Guest 369', it said. At least that much was real. So, my immediate task was to deal with the numerous identities morphing my reality and get back to the Backpackers Hospital… And then, hopefully, get straight enough to cope with whatever might happen the next day.

Chapter V
STILL LIFE WITH BITTEN APPLE

There's a new artist in town, a pensive poet, named Mr Salvador Aldí. There's not much in his appearance to remind you that he used to be a prominent Spanish surrealist. But if you know his background, there are a few things you notice. That said, I did recently see him hungover from Hennessy stumbling not over an empty bottle with the practised eye of a regular drunk, as he trekked up the stairs, lifting his knees high and letting his dirty boots mark the manners of his art on the guacamole green carpet. A highly pronounced footprint, ever looking upward and ever conforming to him who has vanished.

In general, the public approves of Mr Salvador Aldí having been taken on. With a surprising degree of sympathy, people say that the way society is arranged today puts him in an elevated position and for that reason, as well as because of his historical significance, we should be as supportive as possible. Nowadays — this is something no one can deny — there is no artist like Salvador Aldí. It's true that few people know now how to saddle a horse with time; nor is the skill needed to dream extraordinaire wholly a lost art; there are plenty of people who find themselves living a still life with bitten apple, vanishing fast into oblivion and curse Salvador, their father — but there is no one, absolutely no one, capable of leading us to cosmic order. Even, in those days, the gates of paradise seemed unreachable but the direction was given by the higher spirits and further off the machine; no one is pointing the way; it's true that loads of people have smartphones these days, but only to hold eye-contact with the lower self and anyone who tries to follow Salvador with his eyes, ends up utterly bewildered.

That's why it's perhaps best to do what Mr Salvador Aldí has done and bury yourself in the Catalan and Parisian museums. The decision to flee came suddenly; his drafts no longer being gripped by the rider's whip, under lofty lamplight far from the clamour of critics (who live in a digital parallel world, whose capitals are Instagram, Twitter and YouTube), he dreams about our artistic failure.

Chapter VI
HOMECOMING

I've come back, come in over the great sea and I take a look around. It's my family's old hometown. Not really but close. The wind, the eternal playboy, had torn them apart — the puddle and the paddler, drawing circles in xoxolate pudding. Overripe, as if all sorts of funny fruits were falling from the screen, blocking the railway homewards, I strolled, head down, about the station. A torn piece of yellow-tinged paper news, once titling my breath in a game, lifted in the wind. I've arrived. One Kafka with milk, please. What's your name? Chris Mess. Had I eaten from the insane root that takes the raisin adrift? Who's waiting at the high cliffs of speculation, if all reason had been replaced by mediocrity? One coffee with milk for you, sir! There's steam rising out of the coffee machine, they're making milk foam for some Thorsten. Are you travelling or are you here at home? I don't know, really, I don't. Which one of them? It's my father's hometown but each house leans against the next, as if occupied with its own stress, which, maybe or perhaps, I've never cared, or never dared to fully comprehend. Who am I to them, even if I am my father's, the hardworking mechanic's, son? And I don't dare to ask, though, if I am really too numb with fear, or I just speculate in the social distance; I lick my lips and wrap myself in silent wonder. And because I'm so far off, I lost touch, all I feel is my heart throb, or I think I've felt it, throbbing out of my persistent ill-memory. What else have I failed to reckon, if this is a secret known to everyone who can call it a home, who were instigating my rebellion long before me. No. I did this all alone, it's my own delusion. The longer you hesitate to take that train, the more of a stranger you become. What would it be like if someone opened the door and told you that it was all fake, that you've never been a real member of this family in the first place? Wouldn't it seem strange that the train had been blocked for so long, just because you failed to see that home is an unknown destination to a chosen one?

Chapter VII
THE THIRSTY WOMAN

On Thirstday they had killed so many bottles of cava inside the house, that Miss Behave had to vomit the poison out. On the carpet poured the devilish brew and wash it in the sea, because the stench had the humour of all night and nobody was laughing any more. The world had been sorry since Thirstday. Sea and sky were a single pulp.

The ships of the haven, which on summer nights were usually laden with shellfish people, had become a whale of a sad story. The sun was so weak at noon that when Miss Behave was coming back to the house after washing out the vomit, it was summit of her sadness; to see what it was that was reeling and writhing on the slimline in-between beach and horizon. She had to go very close to reckon that it was a tuna fish playing chess with himself, castling clouds (or perhaps she'd to get even closer) — a very gigantic tuna fish, lying sideways in the beach sand, who, in spite of his tremendous flap with the fin, couldn't get back into the water. That is all.

Surprised by that sensation, Miss Behave ran to get wet towels, for help, who were hanging dryly in the kitchen and she grabbed them by the eyelet. Tap: turned on. Her friend, Fanny Tale, stood outside. She looked at the stranded fish with mute stupor.

She was dressed only in a daydream. There were a few curls of hair covering her pearl, tea-tinged teeth in her mouth and her swampy condition of a gin-drenched party girl took away the sense of grandeur she might have had.

The tuna fish's beady eyes, dirty and behung with light sands, were so sad and beautiful, entangled in the what-the-fuck-is-going-on. They both looked at him so long and so closely that Miss Behave and Fanny Tale very soon overcame their sense of sensation and in the end went closer in an attempt to lift him up and take snaps. But that was by all means mad, for the tuna fish was big, bigger, Moby-Dick. Then they dared speak to him and he answered in a Hanseatic dialect with a strong sailor's voice and in brief bubbles. That was convenient as they both thought they were still tripping. With a comical twist and, quite intelligently, they concluded that he was a lonely drunkard from a foreign ship wrecked by the storm. And yet, they called in a neighbour woman — Alina Holiday, who knew everything about the ethereal nature of perception, and all she need was one quick look to show them their mistake.

"He's a captain, a bewitched captain," she told them. "He must have been coming for the golden shovel but the poor fellow is so dry that he must die, if no high tide this way comes any soon."

Having said this, Miss Behave covered the tuna fish with wet towels as best as she could and stood by his side until dusk tugged on her eyelids.

On the following day, everyone knew that a

deceasing-and-gigantic tuna fish was found at the beach near Miss Behave's house. In spite of the judgement of the wise neighbour woman, for whom tuna fish in those times were fleeting symbols of a spiritual change of route, they did not entirely give up hope to rescue him. Miss Behave watched over him all afternoon from the kitchen, amid rhubarb cake and oven mittens and before going to bed, she splashed tap-fresh water onto his primitive scales. Quarter to midnight, when the rain began to drip down her windowpane, Miss Behave and Fanny Tale, nightly-driven by sinister signs and symbols, were killing cava afresh. A short time after the tuna fish made a tremendous flap with the fin, producing a limp sound and with a desire to eat. Then they felt the need to breathe a fresh breeze of life into the dying creature and decided to slip the tuna fish on an inflatable raft with ample of organic soap and purified water and provisions for three days and leave him to his fate on the raging seas. But, indeed, when they went out to the beach with their torches, they found the whole neighbourhood taking selfies with the tuna fish as they watched him dying. Some of them were poking him with twigs into the eyes and gills, having fun with torturing the tuna fish, without the slightest reverence, tossing him all sorts of plastic waste, as if weren't he a spiritual creature but a despicable refugee from hell.

Herman Earnestway arrived quarter to nothingness, alarmed by the strange news.

By that time, a wild discussion had broken out and the mob made all kinds of malicious statements about the spiritual creature. The poorest among them thought that he should be named head of the universe. Others of freakier mind suggested that he should be put into a taxi to the Milky Way. Some creative entrepreneurs hoped that he could be pitchman on the local fish market. But Herman Earnestway, before becoming a literary starfish, having been a hardworking fisherman, knew of their cynical view on the tuna fish's intelligence. Standing by the tuna fish, he reviewed his years lost by the minutes turned to dust and instantly asked Miss Behave to open the shed so that he could take a look at the golden shovel among the fascinated pigs. It was lying in the corner, brightly lit, shining ex sunlight, among the other farm tools and breakfast leftovers of the livestock. Unaware of the cruelties of the world, produced from ancient gold to dig deep in the dirt of long-buried memories, it possessed the magical power to unearth the truth (beyond Wikipedia) of what it takes to finally be you and loved, despite yourself. Herman Earnestway lifted his gifted eyes and murmured something incomprehensible in his whitening beard. "It's no sense in helping him," he announced. The free-ranging pigs looked at his melancholic countenance, when he lay down the golden shovel very softly, as if it were a baby put into the arms of a mother. Then he noticed that haunting smell of manure dispersing from under his boots and maggots were gathering by his soles. A grave coldness tugged on his shoulders. And then he came out of the shed. Well, crawling on all fours to warn the humorous against the risk of being too curious and to confuse the sincerely intended. It's hard to say what must have happened in the shed. However, suddenly the mood was splendid like a field of poppies. He argued philosophically that if scales were not the characteristic covering of fish, in determining the difference between tuna and turbot, they were even less so in reckoning reality. Nevertheless, he promised to write a letter to the University of Maritime Affairs Professor, in order to get a final insight from the experts.

His prudence recovered one's wooden leg. The news of the stranded tuna fish, living now in a customised basin, being fed herring and mackerel, weren't but the old news but spread with such rapidity that after a few hours, the beach had the bustle of a Beatles concert in the '60s and they had to call the cops to disperse the mob that was about to knock the house down. Fanny Tale, her spine twisted from sweeping up so much plastic waste, then got the idea of fencing the popular beach area and selling beers, charging one haiku admission to see the tuna fish. She'd always liked to dream about fishing for tuna fish. Now, as the seas were almost entirely depleted, she thought of it as the most poetic thing to do, for it was so sad and beautiful at the same time.

The creatures outside of the fence, who lacked the ability to write a haiku, looked from tuna to man and from man to tuna and from tuna to man again; but it was impossible to say which was which in the end.

Chapter VIII
FOUNTAIN OF YOUTH

If unknown waters are the Fountain of Youth, sail on.
 — Max Fresh

Got access.

Must check, what's left. Dimly lit.
 Cold, old tobacco smoke.

A door, front right. The walls, all unwhite. Hanging near door, his face to infinity — A Portrait of a Survivor of the Yolocaust.

Left back, corner, large window, curtains down.

Floor wet, almost slipped; four eyeballs met, covered by an anxious lid.

In the rear, an armchair, glued to desk, hidden behind the screen, Ole Unwell's melancholy.

Motionless by the door, his eyes fixed on Ole Unwell, Fresh took his bag and left.

Behind, a bunch of books, the concept of time and a foul state of mind. Put into the oblivion box, the lid on.

Lived on, water fresh and yet…

It is worse, much worse, than you drink. The soberness of climate change is a fairy tale, perhaps as drunk with ignorance as those who think it's not happening at all and comes to us, bundled with fall-apart delusions:

That global warming is an Icelandic saga,

That wealth can be shielded against rising waters,

That burning fossil fuels is the price to pay for continuous economic growth in a crisis that is Nada. The. Devil. Wears.

Horseshit.

None of this is true. Just born afresh.

Standing, in my cucumber-cool apartment and, mixing unique design with comfortable seating. Beyond trends, it's Fresh who lives here now. And wow, look how focussed he is on dropping deadweight to elevate and quantum-writing his reality sane… Slow as the green giant snail but with magic lines spiralling up into a higher dimension of self. Firmly, Fresh glanced into the mirror and repeated: Why am I so happy, talented and smart? Why am I so healthy, young and strong? Why do things always work out in my favour? Why do I love and cherish myself, so much? Why is my life so happy and harmonious? Why do I deserve wealth and success?

Altered stage of consciousness: The Bird View.

Don't know how Eye got here. Perhaps, that is beyond maybe, in a dream-like night out, an affair with two bohemian girls from Denmark or Sweden or both —

Swemark or Denden; certainly, they got the keys of some kind. Eye was helped. Eye'd never have got here alone. Either they'd slipped me the ticket or hinted at the correct numbers: positive thought + expectation + belief. The cup of epiphany was filled to the brim with desires. That's Life: a game one must play, so why not have some fun, meanwhile? One shall have detachment. One shall visualise with acute exactness. One shall believe. One shall feel all right. One shall not forget to smile. Truth is, Eye'd won the lottery jackpot: big time! Symbols of a slumbering elephantasy awakened in the wealthroom. Bought a splendid apartment. Back in Copenhagen, on vacation, Eye'd learned to envision the desired outcome with faithful precision. It worked!

My new home is not too big and not too small. A cosy melange of tender sofas and so far, undiscovered artworks of revolutionary ripeness. At the stuccoed walls that each stood erect against pioneering powers, Eye hung them up — the poetic flowers from my lost love — perhint, were interpretable as a ship driven ashore by the wind's uncertain hands. Why? iDunno, why.

First, thinking - thirst. Drink: down poured the, second. Pelting gin with gelato, melting. Eye think a cheeseblue would do well on the walls; or pantherpink like used in prisons to calm inmates.

But back to our question: Why did we part? Who?

You and Anna. Eye guess Eye loved our petit dinners and the way we carried ourselves with utter kindness and calming caress in tune with each other's music. Good times, still muse on it. So, what had happened?

Surrealistic trumpets silenced by a sword within. The

music was stopped before the grand melody had begun. Flung myself out into the unknown, for fear of losing the freedom to… Eye had to leave for the sake of the arch-cheating dream that haunted me, like the uncertain nature of nature.

Flames at my feet, sufficiently ignited and set aflame in the psyche, quenched by teardrops. Sat down by the wonderful window with the landscape behind. Rising ashes. Another climb upon: Mount Tipsy. The re-ascent. From ashy to witty.

Hence, a new star was born: Max Fresh — The Wizard of Deliberate Creation.

Once at the top of the rocky hills of thought, which emptied in the River Cum, Eye saw my spirits mounting. This pure world found then, up and above, was a land alit. All around, rose petals rustling with satisfaction. Fresh's state of decay lent colour to this view. Seductive melodies of sexual ecstasy entered the neighbours' unsexed ears through faith-bricked walls. The branded neighbours, enflamed with curiosity, kindled a candle of interest. They wanted to know who the new magnetic stranger was. Ding Dong. "Good-die, Mr…"

"Fresh. Max Fresh."

"Yes, of course, Mr Fresh. May Eye ask for an egg?" "My husband will come along next Tuesday and bring you a new one."

A well-known way to welcome a stranger in hope of an impromptu party. Eye surrendered to that claim like a candle's flame to the wind. "Come to my cave, in which the mid-class metamorphosis continues, continues to transform the façade of the everyday lie. Die in mediocrity, or live in abundance. Everybody was invited: high society, low society, bro society, no society, animals, plants, cans, bottles, models, models with bottles and bottles with cracks, as well as all sexes. You shy?"

"Nay, Eye'll consider it — bye," said Miss Behave mischievously and then, "Before Eye forget — would you like to introduce yoursex?"

"Sure. Eye [am] Eye — now, new, nower. Alive. While we all are dying under the illusion of disconnectedness, crumbling like crisp croissants under pressure from above. So, there isn't time to grow old or such displeasures. For which," Eye said (subtly peeking at her décolleté), — "Come, come tonight to my cave and snack on the everlasting biscuit, if you aren't a professional misfit. We shall drink, play and laugh and maybe more… And, when you go home again it will be dark. A suspended, dangling darkness. A cocoon of smartened ignorance, in which we shall sit, seduce and seclude each other, before the moon hatches another relic of the past. A hidden star in a cocoon of social separation. Protected from the harsh realities of must-dos, must-haves and must-sees; must cease to cohere to an outdated ideal. Must mutate. Must procreate like eels in a unified field of energy. Must trust in the rigorously authentic metamorphosis of the butterfly — loves first, steps out and learns to fly."

"Beauty, beauty!"

Miss Behave went back inside her flat with an anticipatory smile on her face, knowing that this stranger had a special energy that made her emotions skyrocket, as if little airplanes were taking off in her stomach.

But still, even in this fresh garment of gayness, the questions remained persistently:

Who am Eye?
Why am Eye here? What's One League?

Eye faked it through the day with somehow Johnnie walking in the red, like most bank accounts after the grand pandemic. Why did inequality persist, albeit the majority wanted peace and freedom? Ask yourself the answer. Question the question.

Left, corner of the attic, Fresh, near desk, a bottle of red.

Behind, a bunch of books, images of past intentions.

Down, pearls of water, curled along the bottleneck.

At level, met, the tablecloth, wet.
Old ends, get loaded, got pretty, outmoded. Upon silence, embarked.

Altered stage of consciousness: The Frog View.
Mostly thoughts of isolation, anxiety and depression. Wondered whether she must have thought of me too at the self-same moment, simultaneously, you know — twilife — some sort of telepathy may have occurred. At least some signal was sent, Frog-Eye was pretty sure of that. And yet, Frog-Eye was depressed — in need of deep rest. Frog- Eye had been waiting for so long to see her again but didn't and Frog-Eye missed her terribly. Or was

that ego-illusion? Ask nature! A cunning fox in the burrow, twisting together love, lust and loss. Shot dead. Anyhowl.

In the Now. Jacuzzi. Champagne. Pants off. Highday night, pre-housewarming, Frog-Eye swept up the dust of social anxiety and formed it. In came the first party guests like brief bubbles into a glass. A bee's bathtub. Needles of champagne tickled on the tongue. Needless to say, that Frog-Eye felt strung out and thin like a needle in the hay — without some strong to drink, to break the ice.

Petúr, Gareth, Gilcade and Miss Behave were the first to arrive. It was a sloppy party at the start. Vice-ridden talents, sitting in the jacuzzi, sipping on Singapore Slings or hiding behind tablets to postpone the inevitable overcoming of social insecurity. Hosting: a lemon, a pinch of salt, a tequila, a halt, a spin, a frog-jump into bad habits. Frog-Eye was trapped in a world made of sin.

Since Frog-Eye couldn't fathom why it was so lively, libidinous and lethal at the same time, Frog-Eye went on carousing. To get drunk, that is, to be tied to a lullaby, listening on repeat. Cheers to the crying clown, sitting on the half-moon, dangling down his feet with his toes tipping into the margins of consciousness. Thanks for the party, Frog-Eye needed it for finding his arty essence.

Semantic suit, for sale, worn once. Originally bought from MS Fond of the Bottle.

Frog-Eye was frowned upon by his former self. Another state of mind: taken on and on and on. Consciousness, also called the A, B, C of a quantum writer's profession, transcended. A real quantum writer derived words from the muse, finessed the individual view of omnipossible worlds and tessellated truthpaths through Newtongue.

All was still, except a stomach's grumble. Frog-Eye looked out of the kitchen windough, kneading out the scene. Green meadow with a fluffy feel to it. Amid animated buttercups and nature's rural solitude the flowers of fancy were all abloom. Here, before the sunset gun, changed my name amoon.

Boom. Next morning. The postman snapped shut the post box. An entourage of letters arrived. Packed with words, such as mule or mensch, carried loads of information to further the agenda of The League. But that was about to change profoundly.

That being said, he got tired of hanging around, and desired to breathe fresh air. Went outsane — better than going insane!

The grass's hairdo fatal to horses, dogs and mowers, though tolerated by the ass, happened to cushion the latter. Fresh sat on the green meadow with a grant cinnamon bun placed on a napkin like a price, writing one-handedly a famous letter, tapping into the subconscious, in which a deep dive Frog-Eye took. A fairy tale: Kiss a frog to connect to another world: The observer observing the pond of his cosmos.

Thoughts, symbols, subsumed in semantics, while Frog-Eye plucked poetic flowers in Daisy Garden —

that's when Fresh's face hardened with suspicion. Wisdom from a daisy: she loves me, she loves me not. Such is the rapidity of thought.

Peaceably pursued the pathless path on foot. In consequence of a natural need, Frog-Eye peed freely amid the brilliant bushes by the lake, pacifying the penis — no, bladder. Felt better then, like a clitoris. Hands washed in the water. Two sketches (a bird and a frog) floated on the surface like fake news distorted the history of information was disagreed upon. Then, shot a photo for Insta. Zombie life. Dead already?

Twelve o'clock at Carnivore Cross, any waiter knew that lunch leaned at the doors of perception, as Max Fresh held a hot dog in his hands in hostage. Sizzling sausage. To forget future and past for the sake of satisfying the stomach in the now. Why?

Beginnings and ends. Circular path: growing infinite. Now, know how… All is behind you.

Fresh loved it when ordinary acts like eating sausage tamed the monkey brain.

Rested then by an old oak and was rocked into a deep dream, because all was still, interpreted by an ill-qualified Frog-Eye, transformed by the brain into words; sonic sequences that shall convey meaning through frequent airstreams directed at other animals. Submissive illusions streaming through a series of sounds and symbols. Tied up into a poetic parcel. Click. Edit. Sent. Prompt delivery:

Horses are tied by the head, Dogs are tied by the neck
And men by the mind.

Less or more wild: all animals. A bunch of hairs (or none) distinguished them, combed by the poetic promptings of present perception.

Arrived at the park appeared ghost-quiet, except for

the rustling leaves and the gentle wind. A giant snail keenly pursued its path on the grass green. Slow, anxious and isolated it seemed to be. And yet, a snail comes out of the house to put out her feelers, to host impressions of everyone and everything. No prejudices, no masks, no bullshit. That's fucking courageous! Slowly sobered up.

But Frog-Eye, why am Eye feeling this way? Why am Eye seeing this way? Why am Eye thinking this way? Who or what conditioned me to behave in a manner that is destructive to my inner peace and happiness? Who had implanted this voice in my mind?

The ghostly breath of a lawyer, who perhaps was, or percosts wasn't there, suddenly startled him. At once, Fresh went back to the house in the name of swiftness. No applause was given. The apartment door on floor four was tilted open but somehow, Frog-Eye could not enter, because all was still. Not a kettle's whistle. From the neighbour's chimney the smoke rose rich and rife. None but suspended sounds — the glowing pistol on the ground, a rake on vacation, a distant inflatable flamingo in the neighbouring house's swimming pool; belladonna lilies on the balcony of someone's beloved affair, [insert your name]. All was still, not a thistle's murmur.

And cakes, of course, blackberry cakes and strawberry cakes with whipped cream, their zeitgeist so sadly dying. Vanquished by the heat of consumption. Leaving afternoon's high for the kushes' glow. Contentedly, Frog-Eye inhaled the scent of the AK47 was a high calibre among the weeds. So far, so high! Then a mysterious man knocked on Fresh's ears and came into Fresh's head that seemed dead empty and walked along the nasal corridor searching for sympathetic sounds. Frog-Eye knew him well, he had the swag of a bag, potatoes wrinkling handed him a facial note inkling of a node of autumn in the heart. No words were exchanged as if the gaiety of their past companionship had been reduced to a spectre. Both turned their heads defiantly away a grey cloud modified the mood of the moment is all Frog-Eye has. Perhaps it's time to let go at last.

Enigmatically, Fresh smiled, for suddenly he knew he had won the love of his life back in a lucid dream; and yet, all his previous efforts to enter such world seemed to subsume in an escape, a psycho-semantic blockage made of codes, symbols and secret societies gnawed on his faith of actualisation. Yes, his love for her was still latent… Breeding ideas of a reunion. And those ideas spread virally like a wildfire. You breathe in, as you breathe out.

Breath of Fire

Anna, Eye just want to look at you, look at a beautiful ghost —
　Never too far from you and never too close.
　And then Eye want to close my eyes,
　When you walk out of my life, And you never come back again but Eye won't care,
　Because Eye got the best of you and the best will always be there — the lift of your velvety lips,
　The bliss of our very first kiss,
　Oh, how Eye got impressed by you when the sense of magic appeared and the scent of you.

And the way you felt —

Anna, Eye got the breath of you and it is mad with love like hell.

A flirt between pain and gain bugged his game. Eyelids in surrender mode. Couldn't sleep, though. The wildfire-like chaos in the mind wouldn't allow it. And then, again the primal urge to find out.

Altered stage of consciousness: The Ape View.

Who am I, really, a matter of definition — a man with horse and machine or a man with heart and machete? Who'd YOU rather trust? Well, first I will tell you who rather not to trust —

General stupidity! General stupidity is to be found in bars... and there he was, two steps back, sitting, surrounded by art décor and a ghostly girl, sipping on a Negroni with her — Miss Behave knocked out the clock of caring. They talked and talked and talked amid beers and bitches with the beaver. She told him that the beaver was in vogue. "She who's a believer, cultivates a beaver." They flirted outrageously in front of the other barguests like frivolous friends. Hence, I looked at the liquors behind the bar, somehow absinthe-minded. Hastily her hands fumbled with a pale piece of paper.

Swiftly put back into her bag. The re-activation of the monkey mind. Was Miss Behave a spy? Was she sent by The League?

"May I kiss you?" Miss Behave asked after a silence. And yes, their lips met, with a cracking chemistry... like pork roast. Immediately, Fresh knew that it was more show than amore. What was it good for, then, to spend your time pretending? Why on earth was everyone pretending to know what was good for someone, if they didn't even know what's good for themselves? More than seven billion perceptions and (almost) every one of them self-righteous. Where's thy mind at?

Human relations are liquid, they have ripples, ups and downs like waves. Fresh's eyes filled with a silver shine. All those years he had kept her close to his heart; his love for her felt so real and yet surreal. All those tears — what a waste of time… A concept that kept being an illusion constructed by the mind.

I to the world am like a drop of water, that in the ocean seeks another drop who, falling through the strainer of time, must venture forth forever.

After reading this, I thought that I never want to think again; never even drink again. And still, next weekend was coming as certainly as tides. So, I decided: Life is too short but I live for you!

So, listen, I made a decision and went back to the house, in sobriety pulled out my pen and wrote it all down, as it REALLY happened.

Altered stage of consciousness: The Heart's View.

It was Showerday, the day after Highday. A torrential rain ran down along the windowpane. It was Showerday. It was not raining. The party was long over. Horribly hungover, I recapped with a certain clearness of vision — to tell the truth, it is some considerable time now since I last knew what I was talking about. It is because my thoughts are ever whistling a merry tune. I am therefore immune to a shrinking in spirit; I've plenty of time: no fomo, no limits. Innit logical to praise the moment? As all we have followed by a simple desire to check ye phone and respectively succumb to a state of numb. Oneness shall await us at the end of all endurance.

To hell with endurance, I'll say what I am but first I will say what I am not, then what I am. I am neither Max Fresh, nor Known, nor MS Fond of the Bottle, nor — no, I can't even bring myself to name them, nor any of the other innumerable figures I'd sported, who told me I was they, or this, or that. I must have tried to be, through fancy, or through fear, or to avoid jumping out of the mirror ('holder of the shadow') and be at leisure, at least for once — in symbiosis with the higher self.

Perhaps it's by trying to be Known that I'll finally succeed in being me. Hadn't thought of that before, or had I?

Dreams. Deliberate creation. Simple math, you see: faith times pi. Sixteenth letter in the Greek alphabet. A transcendental number. Celestial counterpart of the sun's getting hotter, as it loses heat. Life's like a fleeting fireball — it burns as you fly and it flies along. But why, why the frog then was it all like it was?

"Gravid," he kept repeating, "gravid." Danish for pregnant. "The laws of gravidity, first formulated by Newton, now rectified by the immortal Jon Known. God said, let there be Newtongue and there would be Love without Fear." He roared with passionate laughter as the lime tree alley narrowed his view into telewisdom.

At the dim lines of perception, hallouminative lamps drew a new pathway. He looked at the laborious lanes of his past and remembered another night, years ego, aboard a ship, when there were no lights in the dark and the seas beneath the cog were totally indifferent to his art. He had walked up this path alone, full of melancholy emotions which, though the cause of them was different, were resembling the same melancholy emotions which swelled within him tonight. Right. He was helped by higher spirits. He had been most madly in love. But where was his love now?

That's when his random walk seemed to come to an end. He glanced at a strangely familiar Old Oak at a strangely familiar pond from his dreams and the silhouette of a farm in the distance. Far off the small village, where he had started to journey into the unknown, out of affection to an unknown love within, he must have walked on and on and on, until he stumbled upon — Anny Ivy and the thought of their separation depressed him quite. With tears swelling in his eyes, he looked about:

Stabling for horses in the stalls,

Stabling for humans in the attics of thought.

Digitally controlled and manipulated by voidoscopes (re-wiring the users' brain circuitry through dopamine release, producing highly addictive feedback loops for the sake of keeping their data slaves content). In the arch-cheating shadows of global tech corporations and a financial elite, you could imagine yourself at the entrance of Platon's allegory of the cave — click, edit, enter — and you found yourself in front of a portable prison cell, cementing the current belief system.

Between the broad, suicide doors for cattle were littler doors for humans — constructed by The League. But The Doors of Perception to omnipossible worlds, which thus neatly knew how to interrupt the flow of his inspiration, stood ever open.

And, Fresh pondered another exit:

Who is not spared to dive into the frog-jumped pond, need to speak, to think with thoroughness and care, to know where one is, where one was, during the wild dream, up and above, under the stars, dogs chasing ducks in parks, near ponds, crumbs of memories were flung, venturing forth in parts and particles. The invention of the human separation was manifested in two tangent hearts, to beat on: DaDum, DaDum.

Apart, A part,
A syllabic arc,
Eye am big foot — Drumbeat of the heart;
At last, a very valuable thought: Life is short,
Art is anaconda,
But I will live for you as long as it lasts: Love.

Chapter IX
BREAD FOR THE WEIRD

They say there's no knead to explain the best bread in the world. You'd taste it. Wak - wak! Though, I really like Meyer's sourdough, I love the way it smells.

Having said this, he started to increase his pace, darting away and, upon reaching the duck-dense pond, he crumbled into a thousand fish pellets and the ducks looked at it with disgust, cackling like geese.

"Geesus," exclaimed a young boy, turning to his friend, pointing at the pile of fish pellets.

And the sun continued to shine, as ever and stately sunflowers nodded with their heads approvingly.

Chapter X
ANNA IVY

THE THREE O'CLOCK hurried out of West Cross but he was neither drunk nor high, this time, to Potsdam. A grinding sobriety made arid the corner of the first-class carriage in which Chris Mess was sitting with... His thoughts were like a quick lizard zig-zagging in a desert of infinite sands, with no oasis in sight. Once amore, he fumbled in his jeans pocket, brought out and unfolded the fragile paper. Once more he read.
    How many times had he read it before?

Shall I meet my dearest poem in the sight of you?

Mess had loved her madly, Anna Ivy, who was younger and prettier than he, although it was entirely possible that during the past five years or so, no wait... Shame, it was already six, her radiance had vanished like his top hair, who knows? In a few minutes we shall find out. Mess had left Copenhagen and Anna remained, if at all. In fact, you might say that it was Mess who had been left, while Anna, a recent graduate of Art School, thought of nothing but her canvas and was tempted to mark everything besides with the boring-stamp... How loud, how loud he heard his heart pound, as he knew in a few minutes she would come in. The thin thread of his lifeline (thrown to save him from drowning) seemed to break by contemplation of the trivial... Was an embrace or a kiss called for? The train approached the platform. Here the station changed its name and a new life began.

There had been a messenger message that Monday morning and an anonymous writer had announced in Danish that she wanted to meet, if he would be talking to her about the secret agenda of One League and that would of course, mean that his life was in great danger. How did they find out that he had accessed the sacred chamber of knowledge? This had come as a surprise, even though, Mess already knew that the highest members of The League sent people, people who spied on him, people that followed each of his steps, since his arrival in Berlin. Yes, Mess had a friend who had a friend, who knew in turn a man who worked in the bookstore: Another Shakespeare.

Anna had come on an assignment to arrange the purchase of something or other. Was it possible that she had anything to do with the secret of One League? More than six years! A feeble flame had flickered in the unknown and at a glance into her eyes, would turn either to ashes or spring the true Promethean fire. Mess mediated to inquire into the extent of the corruption of yet unconscious resistance.

Oh, tell me mo' about Anna Ivy! I want to hear all about Anna Ivy. Well, you know Anna Ivy? Yes, of course, we all know Anna Ivy. So, tell me mo'. Tell me now. Tell me all. You'll die when you hear. I don't care. Tell me. Well, you know, when the yung horse went wildly obscure and did only what he desired, following the drumbeat of his heart? Yes, I know, go on. Wash quiet and don't be douching. Tuck up your sleeves and loosen your truthtape. And don't walk me Nordic — hike — when it gets to you! Or whatever it was they tried to make out of the Summerstriking in the Unwoods. He's an awful yung wrida. Look at the jens of him, totally R.I.P. Look how dörty he is! He has all the mud on the midfield of his back like a macaque. And it's seeping und solidifying since the concept of time went welk. How many degrees is it I wonder? I washed it, the supreme sweater in the green machine. Geometrical hallucination characterised by regular lines and shapes. I know by heart that the drumbeat goes on, daDUM, daDUM! Scotch in my hand and starving my soda to make my private love public. Escaping soma. Water it well with the uncanny can and then clean it. Ye meanings are heavy rubber to Harvey winestains.

And the mind map of wetlands and the Ganges of sin in it flowing! What was it he undid her tits for on Sunday Circus? And how long was the bow rudder of the cog? It was put in the niches what he did, niceties and piers of pleasure, the King Horse with sillyphus distilling, thusly sipping on the vines of separation. Time's slipping away.

Now know people will accept poems as payments. They whale until death calls time upon the tale. Untamed tombs 'til will fills the well of youth to the brim. Live forever: humans are meant to. Consult a bible. It shows: reality is a liquid matter. As you drink, you shall be. Turritopsis nutricula jellyfish. Oh, the thirsty yung wrida! Far off the office. Herr Traunsesich bitte ins Büro — shot dead! And, brainwashed by the cut of cake! And, the spill of lake! And, Harvey winestains on Floor Fem, outbalanced the karma account! How he used to hesitate to take that toffee from CFO Horst Horse, the famous elk gallop zum Späti bei Nacht and Wind, with a hiccup of grandeur on his childlike curiosity spring, dreamydrip on the surface of things, like a broken umbrella leaked London. Ask the Riders of the Storm or Boi Lyn Water or the Kid with the Panini stickers for answers. How elster is the unhatched egg? Wild salmon? Hugs of climate change signed by Earlyflower? Or Kafka in the Kitkat Club? New Hempshire, Turnheel on the Marryme? Who nested in Adam and Eve's Tree of Knowledge or suggested sin by Bottle, Captain Fond of the. For me too neither knocked the nugget. And by wildgaze Eye thee gather. Flowers of Mount Tipsy on the brink of untamed time, makes wishes and fears for the happy kissmust. She can show all her curves, off course, licence to play. Not a lobsterphone to ring her but an angstcrop growing along the river of palm, deserting the pen. In unknown waters he barged it, the boat of love, borrowed from the harbourless Grasshippie, 'til timedragged marks sparked the fire of his words aflow with faithfornication and he loosened two Keynesians from under his tilt, the grand Phallic rover pensioned. By the scent of her clover, they made the wild punbath. Supersocks pulled over his face. But where was Himself, the Hamlet, the… hang on…

Bubbles, on my voidoscope, it's Boi Lyn Water, so rarely thought of, the implications of taking up his true calling.

When they say, they saw him saving the whale, no

wait: the tunafish. "Don't do it, 'twould cut you in two!" He earned the grand comeback hard, our MS Fond of the Bottle, the drunk quantum poet. Well, well ejaculate your calibre and tell me mo'. Her grapefruits were sweetripe and juicy her plum, rendered with reinheit. Sum and a part of the whole, preached a pond for a prince. Sparrownotes and pigeonpoetry beside. Tune your heart and fall into amore, you are born enuff and nothing short of, hence. So long as the lucksmith finessed his craft, wait patiently! Look at Heinz, the Beansman, still baked. And yet, Live forever? Yes, you can, like beer. Take two and peer into the wet of her wonderstruck eyes, daymuse and nightnurse but a fire, for a shopping spree in Berlin City aglow. Don't you know, he was cult a boy of the brains. Bumbleblizzard in the chic beaver boutique, frozen glances, so that she was away with the buzz of her phone! Once herring swarmed together, now lonely erring in the ocean of sigh. Who's Anna Ivy? Do you know she was searching for Bottle all around the globe, to go with her, the continuous hope handicapped their reunion, after the big stomp silenced their sound attraction, the elephantastic consoling? She was? Gotta puke. Mood, as hard-boiled as Easter eggs, when he paid the bill for the fine feast in La Boomerang. We will meet again.

Oh, tell me, tell me all, I want to hear, how lit she was in the lift, the staircase, at the suicidal door; a trembling lip, her wonderful saint-like hair combing a lion's mane straight. Things go in circles: a love, a lust, a loss, a lust, a love, a last! Living on, she didn't care, gone is gone, me absentee, after the burning voyage, bon fantasia. Sure, she can't find again a game as good, a gain like moi. Sure, she can't! Thumb on thistle. Heart to wax. Toes on live coal. Well, I don't ever hear the like, but be fond to your loss, mate. Tell the mower. Trim the Grasshippie. Tell the straw of mind that pokes in the eye like war.

Well, old Bottle was as brief as broken boots, with the ship at the shore and the hips of the core of his spleen shuffled and neither benchmen nor herdswhore abroad and tales alit on the crest of riches and nera lamb in the kitchen with lunch, in mushroom without spending cap round Witcoins's great innovation of unconscious content, pained to pore upon a book to seek the light of truth - the great tribute to the giant snail all-wise in the grass green; checking the depths in that land of blades, hunger-striking all alone by humblebee's bed, humming, holding, her picture high on himshelf, a reflection cast a magic spell, forever haunted by retrospectre. Go home Gatsby! You'd think all was dudu in the supreme radiance of the rare flower of hers. And yes, there she was, Anna Ivy, she daren't catch a wrinkle of nostalgia, curling like morning dew from a ruby red rose petal, Endofwant, a wave away only. In a Midsummer dream and Himalaya cheeks, she remained unreachable, unsmiling, silent like the mountain, wandering along heaven's plateau. With Seine and Douro and Spree underneath from his uncertain meander. And at odd time she would look up and bloom all over his countenance as an omnipotent desire tugged her into his flow.

All those years they had been out of touch. Mess knew absolutely nothing about Anna and Anna knew next to nothing about Mess. A couple of uncoupled times

Anna caught a glimpse of Mess's name through the broth of the screen of the social media scene that she dominated with aesthetic genius at will.

And Mess, who had finished his studies with a puzzling paper at the University of Copenhagen, was now seeking his fortune in Berlin, without ever really being able to decide where that fortune lay: in dealing with various copywriting jobs, as his material friends advised, or in attempting to publish the first considerable work of quantum fiction, as inner-self suggested.

By earth and the cloudy quest that so badly wanted to have a reunion of onion and eye and a cry at that!

For the heavens I have so much love and a broken heart, so it is, sitting in bars, dancing in clubs and waiting at cool cafés des arts, for my Danish heroine to peel another layer of the oniongoing misery, my life on a dead swallowship in full sail; my bird nest of our forest of rhetoric; my much-altered morass; my unsandalled feet in sun-heated sands; my fool to the last attempt, to wake up out of this wild daze and bring to horizon an ancient colour I used to wear.

Chris Mess watched through the dreamwebbed window he kept wide open in his faithbricked house. Out, out and away went tessellating thoughts, pondering possible paths, dark tears in the deep gulf between their hearts with their landlocked portion of sea opening through a strait. Asleep with fine dreams on dull hays of bronze and gold, alfalfa or clover, on grass patches, to mow and cure the overgrowing hour: resistance.

Born all in the dust settling at his feet, pale specks of fire, evil eyes peeking thru thy multidimensional fire.

Where fallen stars flung the points of time far into the inevitable gravitation toward each other. A fall of ripe walnuts; brain left, brain right, nag the muse and forget her. Right?

There she danced upon patterning pebbles, where great horses stood by the river with fiery money-manes inflamed the nightwash. A poet, commonly kept as a pet in the mind for those occasions, sat on a woodpile in the wild that wasn't there, sipping from a small vessel with pouring lip and eyed her. A long and a lone intoned groove kept them apart. Once more, she danced, from hip to hip, she's spherical, like a globe, provoking marvellous ships to journey the unknown. I to the world am like a drop of water, that in the ocean seeks another drop who, falling through the strainer of time, must venture forth forever.

Old Ruby with a fellow fire, burning within this gemmed point of tie, turned it loveside and held it at the glowing sun by the everlasting cliff of speculation. And then the outworn old jeans from the fornication on the forlorn cemetery re-emerged! The brainsoaked words of a scientist: antithesis. A barrel of guns fronted in your face.

Orient and immortal self-identity exiled in his ego from Tree of Lego to Tree of Knowledge to Weeping Willow. They love laughing, they laugh weeping, they weep smelling, they smell smiling, they smile hating, they hate seeing, they see thinking, they think silence. An inkling of autumn in the heart. Rule of rose and withered weeds of the sheepish fox would that fairgazer spot in the curse of his persistent course.

What bitter's love? Answer: resistance.

He turned and halted by the bend of bay, a black bookcat procured faiths.

"Twopoems each," the levitating black bookcat said. "Four for six haikus."

Tattered pages. A Portrait of a Survivor of the Yolocaust. LOA-Poems — Reality As You Please!

Binding to the divine in men, men in imagination, probably feeling impatient, what is all this? A snake is under cover. Bringing us soon 'Reunion of Matter and Spirit'.

Secret of all secrets. Sealed off the weaklings. They laugh weeping, they weep smiling. Geometrical illusion in your hands: the voidoscope. You got a new text.

Who wrote this? Invocation of the psyche of your soul — to all believers in Newtongue divulged. As good as any other invocation, as humble as forgotten. Flung forth, charismatic like a cold noodle on an unswept floor.

"What are you doing here, Chris?"

He shut the book quick.

"What are you doing here?" Anna said again.

A Shakespeare face of nonesuch William, lovely locks frolicking at his sides. It glowed at the sky as she crouched feeding the fire with leaky sneakers. I told her of Paris, Madrid, Barcelona, Copenhagen, Amalfi and Berlin. Those teasetimes at tindergarten, whose spiritual toilettes were the talk of half the town. Late deepasleep under a layer of handwritten poems, fantasised two highflying birds on the verge of a breakthrough.

"What have you there?" Chris asked.

"You wrote it long ago for me," Anna said, smiling

nervously.

"Is it any good?"

"My memory says yes. Do others see me so? Slow, aloof and sensible to the truth of the shadowmind."

He took one of the scattered papers from her breasts. Master Fond of the Bottle's Rare Flower. Yes.

"What did you keep it for?" he asked. "To learn verse?"

She nodded, reddening and twisting nervously her hair, while he read the verses. Her face showed strong emotion.

"Here," Chris said, handing her the poem. "It's all right, I'm quite grateful for all that had happened between sweet and sour. Mind maggots donut eat the sweet memories. I suppose not all fine memories are gone, though, I shall keep it Gonzo."

"Some," Anna said. "Sorry, we had to…"

Save you from drowning in disarranged dreams. We had to save you from yourself, thus the voidoscope. The League could not afford to let you go. All against real autonomy. She will drown me with her eyes, unparalleled beauty, like… there's no comparison. Lovely ebblanes of sea sands swerving around me, my heart, my soul awash with desire but two words aglow… Everything will change as soon as you remember yourselves again.

Do you remember us? Try to remember, you stupid fool! How we met at Drone, dancing like bee and wildflower in the wind. Those days in the Secret Garden, the poems, your drive to drink, the drowning of the muse. Think! Truth is singular. Try to Remember! Humans weave a complex net of lies, just to drive away all experience that hurt and come to terms with them. Repeat with me: I cannot fear, because nothing belongs to me. We will achieve Peace through Freedom and Freedom through Truth! If she can remember, then so can you.

You breathe out, as you breathe in. Since, you do remember now!

Rare Flower.

Shall I meet my dearest poem in the sight of you? Thy voice attunes light's dimly play,
Where worn shoes charm elegance itself, break grey clouds and smiles shines through. And thou wit adorns ours' pearls.
Nor sun can colour such beings bright,
Nor flowers tell your fine complexion. But fondest veins combine both worlds. Never shall thy fair sight vanish,
Nor uplifting lips lose possession. When you dwell upon lines endless but still, words paint tiniest fraction.
As long time goes and men sensate,
Thy flower blooms and wells with taste.

Chapter XI
SURVIVAL OF THE WITTIEST

You must burn yourself in your own flame, then rise anew from the ashes through quantum change.
— Ray Borne.

Seduced by Miss Amnesia he ran blindly ahead, impetuously turning around for a sec to reconnect with his friends; and abruptly collapsed at a wall on Reeperbahn, Hamburg. Head crash. Hospital. Hippocampus under close scrutiny. Fragmentation of memory. Newborn. Newlife. Newtongue. Who am I? Fell into a deep dream, sensing that one day I would reawaken and take back my rightful place in the community of One League.

Awakening from a severe amnesia… it's like… a land of heaven employed to fly, hugged by an ever-curious appearance, flings himself silently into eternal wonder. His breathing momentwise; but aligned with allowance, intermingling journey towards no spring, no birth, no day, no death, no time, nor sin but immortal self. A pause.

Dream cancels dream in this new realm of thought; subscribed to smile, he died a few times to actually live.

And here we go to gain again a decisive victory over

the omnipotent delusion of our unreliable narrator's whodom.

First thing. Ray Borne sat down at the stable table in his study room and, in a torrential downpour put to paper the Alphapet of Newtongue. 'Twas the ancient, long-forgotten language of One League. All that you see will soon be transformed by the Almighty Nature and other things will be created from this material and again other things will be created from this material, so that the world will always be rejuvenated. Almost nothing is foreign to each other. Everything created is assigned to each other and aims at the harmony of the same world. Perusing his old notes, he looked at things with a fresh pair of eyes, because in that very moment Ray Borne started a new life.

Last but not leaked, here is for you the Alphabet of Newtongue. Last but not leaked, here is for you the Alphabet of Newtongue to help you reconnect with yourself. At first it may seem impenetrable but you will see, it infects you, if you stick to it, it will get you and then… suddenly magic things will happen in your life — you'll be disinclined to think and write differently and, in turn, be able to convey linguistically the message of your real wants and real intentions and real emotions that you have to convey properly, in order to leave behind the capital-conditioned consciousness of our castrated reality and enter the new age of freedom, peace and abundance.

We are somehow prisoners of our ordinary language, enslaved to our flawed system of bad faith and, as a way to escape, Ray Borne created Newtongue: a language that transcends boundaries and breaks with unconscious ties.

Newtongue contains the spirit of freedom to celebrate every moment and appreciate cultural differences, because the members of One League acknowledge the beauty of imperfection that exists in all of us. Newtongue is a language of joy; it gives a voice to those who do not shy away from speaking freely, that is, to speak as you feel and appeal to the whole with wit and the language of the soul. Newtongue is freshness and immediacy; vitality and sparkle. The directness of Newtongue is rooted in its primitivism as a major intercultural impulse in modernity is tied to what is spontaneous, intuitive, simple, untrained, and natural. We are getting closer to our reunion. Resistance proves. The League's Elite doesn't want you to be freed from fear or worry or strife. Don't let The League censor and manipulate your perception of reality any longer. We are at a pivotal point in history right now; from lockdown to liberty to One League. Now is the time to unite. To breathe in love, that is, to breathe out freedom, peace and abundance. To youth, to light.

Alphabet of Newtongue.

1

apples exist; atom bombs exist

2

brackets exist; browsers exist; browsecrastination and butterflow; bingethinkers exist, broccoleague exists, bolognaysayer and badworsewurst exist.

3

chop suey and calamari exist, censorshipwrecked and candleflirt; cicadadas exist; castlecreeps, comeonbear, and covid1987;
  the socabbaged clitverschluss; condominion, cypressnot, the cerebellum

4

douches exist, dreamers, and dullies; dontmarry dullies, and douches, and douches;
  drunken donots exist, drankasip, dayindayouts exist, drankasip and dayindayouts exist; days and death shall have no dominion, undouche, undie, droneaskmewhy, maskyourself, days, death.

5

early fall exists; aftertit, aftertaught and afterAI exist; endlessleep and excelsissi exist; engagemental, enchiladama and eskimono;
  every escargoatcheese eisbegehrt; memorytetris and emojispeak exist; egoslaves, elternatives, and extrasensory perception exist; elderbros, elbeselbow, espressoyourself
  and the fundement, the fundement

6

fish from fischer's fritze exist; foxtrouts and faithfornication

7

agrope is agrope is agrope; genderbender; gettogether; nope, exgoose me hughhef harvey winestains

8

humachines exist; hempkin grasshippies,
    hopkin gracehipsters and pumpkin gymgiants exist; the hitleresque left exists and the green antifart, control

9

instagrammar and instasmell exist; illuminatives exist; ignosaurus and internapional hours exist; the beauty of imperfection exists in opposightseeing; ihike, isnap, ilike exist; illwell, ignoreading and in front of behind exist; the iperspectre exists, and the illegallooking

10

jazz exists; jumpin' jack flash and jpegged jokes exist; jazzdoit like jive,
    jolives, jolips, joyified joeys jumpin exist;
    joggernauts exist; jägershots exist jumping suits, junkie truths and jon known's muse exist; jefferson airplum, justapost away from jane,
    juxtaposed pain to pleasure, johnny walking along

the jellycoast
a jutebag of hipsters exist; justnotnow exists; jealousycircuits exist, and the jazztablishment

11

karma account found; kabeljoy and kill dot com found

12

logophobics in lemonia found; likedensities on fakebook found

13

miss behave and miss fortune found; malmarried to mcmisfit mounting mount tipsy

14

for wish shey found nowtonian time; nihilisted life goals found negated and ninetynine problemmings standing at the cliff of speculation exist; let's go the bed fix, netflix

15

otherwhales exist; oysterwants and orangerover overproduce; the oceans oilways under plasticity and the socabbaged old earth spirits found, hvor
in othernest found oneegg, onedream, oneleague through peacewar and lovehate united

16

probably private property exists;
   polybolig exists; propagandalf exists; perfection perforates perfiction, pocketmind and phomo found, pondering the timebox; and pleasuregrams of pied de pond found;
   putinkerbell found not and the parsley
   absurd penguin sauce; pamela otherways found
   a pile a sugar in mark zuckerberg; pandemicro found; and priesttube shut down for popevious priestporn

17

in quite quizzical quantum quaternary fiction found freedom

18

roomgooglers found; rumgogglers found

19

saunaked saunasians found; serrano sunshine when she's gone fishing; sillyphus distilling soma and the green giant snail found slurpingforward

20

tolkatiff found; toilet paper totalitarians and ticklebutton found; tangotangled threesomeers; twilife, twilit and twiwelk found truthtrimmed; toosammen transdumb, typingponging truthvaxxed facts and textistential tweets found

21

untame usness and uniqueflow, udderly unmilked; unlikelyhut found; undine and uneat smarta;

    200 witcoins earned for minding the unmineable; castaway condom found; convinced of hiv sindom; fitforfuck found not worth menschioning here

22

vinothanks found, vaticanned vampurée,

    verticalifornikkei and the vintage of change found; voguests and evaporridged vitaminecraft found; veni, vidi, visualized vast amounts of vitality; volcancer, vulvarious and virussia found; covidiots, virgini and very valuable vortices found;

    videodorants, vinstasmell and high voltouch found; and the voidoscope, the voidoscope

23

Wit-upon-apps exists; witcoin exists

24

xadnexx exists; xoxolate exists

25

ynot kvestion the kvestion; ynot ask the answer; ymeat, ygather, yme, yother, yread, ybother, yweed; youtubetimetravel exists; yourtubtime exists; and the yummyselfie, the yummyselfie for sizzle

26

the zentury of liberation found meditating; zestcalibre zionsauce found; frank's zipper found; zakabona exists; zusatzstiff exists; the zenith of zapsurdity found scrolling down into zomblivion; there a non-binary zebra visited zoo humane

Chapter XII
THE REUNION

...a path, a lone, a last, a love, along the river's tongue, past Pan and Plato's allegory of the cave, from flood of fjord to meander of mouth, brings us by a deposition of energy in the slack water to a free flowing into the charming sea of Amalfi.

Just getting up now with eyes like bumblebeavers gnawing on the absurdity of the human condition is ageless for the day well soon have the death of will to wiggle lively like the snake in the dungeon of my denim piping down the valley, wild nobody but the grasshippie acknowledged that the community of The League continued its great quest of control as the tide capsised ego's ship one gigantique leak, where the hip birds from the shipherding shore twittered of a new tongue had shorn the sheep of separation, naked now and silent under quarantine the houseless hermit in its search for a new unlikelyhut amud unethical footprints protecting the fresh asset manager slinging foul funds at his opponents. No equality, no man but friend-zoned in the sauna club see how all things hang together like clouds shout out to the man in the ice cream van der weide came a yung bull copulated with a cougar crested rested restless among the fine cattlepillars fell a tree of knowledge from the applemath in the everlasting loophole of the golden ratio calves a quantum particle let me see if i can like beer a dream of nowtonian time it has to do with how you fuel and how you fuse into one ferntastic world of the word obscured by an uncanny tomato very, very peachy indeedy so soft sweet and with an intricate core drop me the sound of praise the oblong dates hath summer all too short this wrap, Ye snack was once the wheat this weed ye smoke was once the seed today is the day of salvation to melt away like dissolved spray the vaporous exultation in the current state — ichi-go, ichi-e, a plum, a pluck, a pleasure.

 Then born enuff a love, a lust, a loss, she shampooed herself with water wet among mud and mad glances from tip of toenail to top of her sail in the unequal countenances. Next, she granted the grove of her keel a peeling with butterscotch crumbling ordinary order pudding-poor legs and humble-headed in the shave grass haute-hipped and her riverflanks falbalablushing behind waterweeds and weeping willows. It was funday, no museday, no friendsday, thirstday, highday, then showerday came around and the green pillow levelled her bronze hair that underscored a point that wanted to wander onwards. Ever vibration she pushed venus's wagon uphill mounting mount tipsy from which she had a tranquil view of the pond pondering clicking cobbles and pattering pebbles the reddest berries and gigglesome gingkoes toeing in the stream at her feet and the gay goldeneye is away with the grayling here a bisexual sailor woo-man fell in love with past, present and future. Describe her once more will you, paint terrestrial spacetime illusion even or odd a shrubbery of shrubs a shrug of bananas a nightwatched lobsterphone thus a sweet xoxolate hhip a rise every morning of standstrong dick a robbing son's cruise so he works the weekends and has it better, One day they will pray stayhome the imperative a guillotine slip for shemale o'shaun a glory hologram born in the promise extinct truthvaccined genderbender that propelled mewe to think for ourselves all that and moorleiche more there over the regnbow shes riding the highest hengst look. Look underneath the dust was growing probing into unknown depths of the human psychology a matter if perceptions fail a plainclothed musician tuning her guitar tar-sharp and feather-flat madammangut two bicycles pedabelle and dr wrongwheel both pros in their fields were despite bikesexuality married to their voidoscopes. Don't be surprised if the editor wheels about on that idea for onesomeness was alltoolonely and novelty furthers complexity that's the key to better dreamlands. The universe shall my father's will then be of no force a pause. Look up Horst Horse blending doubts like clouds meet aircrafts with ramen slurpingforward. Look down Chris Mess a napkin kin of nap listen to thy stomach. Jon Known a thin king thinking crab linguine with chilli call it a cabbage the social median had a brief doze in dreamland quitewhite cowgummi after and beers as many as one can be friends with, when the corona is on top of each breath no swinesnout upon his face and the poor children die of hunger no longer but if that's so ask my solar plexus ape my achilles swell my booty licious flush all formalities wastewaterways answered Salvador

Aldí rapidly rendering the red open doses of famosis in the formose of good grand humours. Quote quixote the truth may be stretched thin but it never breaks and it always surfaces above lies as oil floats on water that is quite about what I came on that mewe mission with mewe intentions laughability to settle with sincerity in newtongue lovecerity ye wisefool. Where are you I'm tired let me be your los angeless vibe thinking I was inkling upon that vice Aldí but what's worth the rhyme without raisin if I cannon make my point jump plus how canoe give it up in the flow thou art's emphasis don't get hooked by phishing or phomo phear not me phear thy phone though so far so,

Impeccable Well
Hear The
Inevitable Air
Bee And Bee.

Another team had entered the league buzzing on the doors of truth in its contribution to create the humachine. They have to behave in certain ways now rules it's constitutional drone. Ask me why peer pressure wanted me to hurry, to marry, to worry and worry and worry even more and more evermore permask them all off course notion rejected straight away, already connected left right left right left right. I love the smell of the flower shop in shower park at its finest primroses and violets first one drop then two drops then tree underneath the ocean. A chineseimpres elm she sought shelter from the pelting rain. "Yes," he said, "I was the rarest flower I'm so happy that we fulfilled our intentions." Once there is nothing like nature in the wild garden drinks from the saharasea and the microwaves rushing and the sky kushing the black raven on the pumpkin fields while pumpkin gymgiants were breaking my bread that once was the oats before the african clock stroke quarter to nothingness and hunger and all kinds of shapes and smells and shoats that would do a good service to the league broke apart and by weaning there is no god who was first the big banger or the universe is a big myth that's odd one big knot like eels mating thanks god morgen freeman left right left right left right little by little turning our attention to what we are really feeling say yes something I often asked its past the bad conscience no lace lasts forever what sneakers shall I wear ah yeah I Nike them gods well or whatever they call themselves will make unwell comments about wetiko go and wash out the coffee stains I said when the pun phone brightly through the kitchen window and when ah they didn't know neither left right left right left right we unmissed the boat at capri lets go said some sort of a 'captain' in his haze-scented khakis when the party was to begin and those fish in the sea swimswamswum as cool as usual and the tourists as cruel as usual dropping plastic waste in tunafish home suddensely alone with the spell the sun shone mad with love like hell and the foxtrees and the figtrouts in the peculiar fernland of words and the sunshat terrasse yes perhaps ah yes and all the guesswork with the daisies and the desires and the douchebags and dire straits flyers red and blue and yellow houses and lemongardens and lavender and marigold and high tide trousers if needed for the last storm longed for the final flood to come along what yes it's jazz piano al dente bred out of the shell like fried eggs and yes for the vegans sausage is no good no food for meat is badworsewurst in the superlative form the only true love of his life he said was I left right left right left right there's no perfect persons right left right left right left and neither one of us were stable in the time why calibrate to all you suggested the stars by a glimpse at the sky and continually becoming it could be something to be around him and wise together comecloser than ever say yes I am in love with the world through the eyes of a girl who's still around the morning after his breathing was faster now many things he didn't know of scavenger p odd and the guy in the coffee shop and the old 'captain' and the opium of his appearance strongly addictive admitted I had to go away and distract from the facts that the endless supply of pleasurable diversions and suicide sods must be DIY sooner or hater separate main quest from side quests drop deadweight then decided to wash up the dishes in the garden around the house and all birds fly and view me coming home very slow one day and the danish dudes laughing gaily in their scarfs as lil hair loss freestyled his parts in the park he couldn't stay any longer tinderdates made him wander off and the poor dogs half asleep in the shades on the grass under the impression of entropy and secret spider webs that knit knowledge and the big sunwheel turning round and round like a pound of butter is how many hours of cow labour idunno and all the neat lidl streets of capri vanished by the bend of bay where I was a rare flower of the mountain when the scent of fresh sea air wafted away crafted salt flowers on the surface of things and how we kissed under the olive bough by the rivers tongue outstretched while the sunset gun fronted in our faces and I thought of that catchy clown in the moon played his tricks well and then I asked him with my eyes heightening suggestibility to ask again 'twas when he'd put his poison arms around me and drew closer so he could sense my big breasts all natural yes and the sun was mad with love like hell and yes he said yes let's be one and forget maybe and live forever and keep being fresh our intentions at least as long as the song plays in the rodeo young forever again knowing who we really are and what we really want left right left right left right suddenly a frog jumped out of the pondering pond from another dimension a prince well yes mewe can webe together for once and once for all is one big lovelottery of spiralling numbers in a kind of blue mood just wait in faith what yes of course so now please say yes I'm in love with the world through the eyes of a girl no matter howclever whatweather whohadher since I met her you do or don't do believe in two tangent hearts who you be with or ain't gonna see through the glassy essence of the mensch of cause now please come to an end yes I am I was and I always will be one world one god one law one reason one truth one force one love forever Anna Ivy.

www.ingramcontent.com/pod-product-compliance
Lightning Source LLC
LaVergne TN
LVHW051954060526
838201LV00059B/3638